NECK IN A NOOSE

The next moment he was sprawling on the floor. He had struck his elbow on the carpet and his shins felt as if they had been kicked. His torch had shot out of his hand as he fell. The crash it made, landing somewhere in the darkness, told him that it had knocked over a piece of glass or china.

The reason for his fall was that he had not seen the downward step just inside the window. But that was not all. As his foot, instead of meeting the floor where he had expected it, had plunged down through nine inches of nothingness, something had struck him hard across the shins.

Neck in a Noose

Elizabeth Ferrars

CORONET BOOKS
Hodder and Stoughton

Copyright © 1943 M. D. Brown

First published in 1943 by
William Collins Sons & Co Ltd
Reprinted in 1993 by Constable and Company Ltd

First published in paperback in 1994
by Hodder and Stoughton
A division of Hodder Headline PLC

A Coronet Paperback

The right of Elizabeth Ferrars to be identified as the Author of
the Work has been asserted by her in accordance with the
Copyright, Designs and Patents Act 1988.

10 9 8 7 6 5 4 3 2 1

British Library C.I.P.

Ferrars, Elizabeth
Neck in a Noose. – New ed
I. Title
823.912 [F]

ISBN 0 340 60750 5

Printed and bound in Great Britain by
Cox & Wyman Ltd, Reading, Berkshire

Hodder and Stoughton Ltd
A Division of Hodder Headline PLC
338 Euston Road
London NW1 3BH

Neck in a Noose

1

At a fork in the road Toby Dyke stopped his car.

The headlights showed him that one of the roads ahead shot steeply upward and that the other road, curving away to the right, skirted the dark hump of the hill before him.

He thrust his head out of the car. He called out: "Hullo there!"

" 'Tis a cold evenin'," answered a voice, harsh with old age and the local accent.

"Perishing cold," said Toby Dyke. "Can you tell me, is there a house hereabouts called Redvers?"

"You mean Toye's place? Ay, straight ahead of you."

"Which road?"

"Whichever you fancy." There came a creak of hinges in the darkness; the speaker pushed open a low gate in the hedge. Beyond the hedge Toby Dyke noticed the limewashed walls and the dim roof line of a cottage.

He asked: "You mean one road's as good as the other?"

"Well, bein' as how you got a car there, maybe you better stick to the left," came the answer. "If you go to the right you miss the hill, but the road don't take you all the way; you got to take the path the last part."

"I see. Thanks."

"You're welcome. 'Tis a cold evenin'."

"Perishing cold."

Toby Dyke set his car at the hill.

It was nine o'clock, a Wednesday, and January. The world was quiet and frozen. From the sharp glitter of the stars in the sky little light reached the furrows of plowed earth in the fields or the stiff, bare twigs in the hedges. The headlights of the car cut a long shaft into silence and blackness.

It was over an hour since Toby Dyke had left London. He had expected the journey to take forty or forty-five minutes, but the car had needed careful handling on the slippery roads, and there had been a patch of fog earlier; then he had missed his way and had had to go back on his tracks a couple of miles. The warmth of the food and drink he had had before leaving had gone out of him. In their leather gauntlets his hands felt chilled.

The engine nearly faded out on the hill. Toby Dyke mumbled curses into the steamy cloud his own breath made before him. Just beyond the top of the hill, where the road flattened out for about a quarter of a mile before dropping again, he caught sight of the painted sign of a bus stop and of several muffled figures. Pines in a gaunt row stood along one side of the road. Driving on slowly, he watched for a gateway.

He found it on his right, almost at the bottom of the further hill. The tall iron gates stood open. As his lights swung over the gateposts he saw the name "Redvers" carved under the stone lions' heads that topped the brick posts. Beyond some trees the roof of the house cut an elaborately jagged patch of solid darkness out of the faintly lighter sky. The drive, curving away between clumpy evergreen bushes, took a wide sweep up to the house.

Stopping the car at the foot of some broad white steps, Toby Dyke tore off his gauntlets, breathed on his numbing hands, and rubbed them together. He eyed the house with some surprise. From the high façade not a single light shone out at him. The walls went up into night, broken here and there only by a faint silvering of starlight reflected from the glass of a windowpane. The house was enveloped in unexpected reserve, in unwelcoming secrecy.

Stepping out of the car, he stamped his feet on the gravel, then tramped up the steps to the door. He pushed at a chromium bell button. Waiting, he took a look round him and up at the coldly shining stars. The darkness was like a drop scene, with spiky silhouettes of leafless trees edging the indigo sky.

After about half a minute he tried the bell again.

Nobody answered the bell and there was no sound of footsteps or of movement within.

But a sound did reach him. It was the sound of a voice talking steadily on and on. It took him a moment to realize that he was listening to a radio announcer reading the nine-o'clock news. Again he pressed his thumb on the bell, kept it there, waited.

Toby Dyke was in the early thirties, a tall man, well-built and wiry, with thick black hair and heavy eyebrows ruled across a long, dark, narrow face. He had a thin beak of a nose and dark eyes set in deep, bony sockets. Inside the turned-up collar of his overcoat his sallow cheeks were drawn with the cold. He held his shoulders hunched and the overcoat huddled round him.

Waiting, ringing, then trying his luck with the knocker, he swore once or twice. Then he tried the door handle. The door was fastened. He waited a moment longer, then abruptly he turned, ran down the steps to his car, groped inside, and from the pigeonhole on the dash drew out a small flashlight. With its pale wedge of light pointing ahead of him, he set off round the side of the house.

Still behind every window he found darkness. From somewhere inside the house the voice of the announcer talked steadily on, and that reasonable, mechanical voice, issuing out of the dead body of the house, began to seem eerie—eerier even than the silence itself.

A second door, leading into a conservatory, was also fastened.

As Toby went on, small lines appeared round his eyes

and something taut and wary got into the way he moved. He tried to open a window; finding the catch resisted him, he thrust both his light and his face close up to the glass.

The room inside was a dining room. A long, narrow table ran down the center. There were paneled walls and a high stone fireplace. In a wide grate, between a pair of ferocious firedogs, the beam of the flashlight picked out a few pieces of burned-out coal in the midst of a heap of ashes.

As he looked at that faded fire the lines round Toby's eyes deepened. He moved on quickly.

At last, at the back of the house, he found an entrance unfastened; a pair of french windows, that opened outward on to a sort of veranda, were closed but not latched. When he tugged at the handle one of the glass doors immediately swung toward him. At the same instant the voice of the announcer seemed to start speaking almost at his ear. The wireless set was just inside the window.

Yet there was no light in the room. Even before Toby had cautiously parted the drawn curtains he could see there was no light within, for not a gleam shone through or round or under the draperies, which had a heavy silky feeling in his fingers.

Switching off his torch before silently stepping into the room, he let the curtains swing together behind him. A small red glow at the far end of the room showed where a fire had burned low but had not yet quite gone out. The room was still warm from it, and the dull redness of the embers lit up dimly the curve of a hearth and a foot or two of carpet.

He stood still, listening.

The announcer at his elbow was talking of a reviewing of troops. Apart from his voice, there seemed to be complete silence in the house. Though Toby strained his ears, not another sound reached him except the faint stirring of the cinders in the fireplace.

Muttering uneasily: "What the hell . . . ?" he switched on his torch again and took a step forward.

The next moment he was sprawling on the floor. He had struck his elbow on the carpet and his shins felt as if they had been kicked. His torch had shot out of his hand as he fell. The crash it made, landing somewhere in the darkness, told him that it had knocked over a piece of glass or china.

The reason for his fall was that he had not seen the downward step just inside the window. But that was not all. As his foot, instead of meeting the floor where he had expected it, had plunged down through nine inches of nothingness, something had struck him hard across the shins.

Sitting up and cursing, he put out groping hands to find what had tripped him. His hands immediately encountered a long rod of metal, and as he slid his fingers along it he found that it was curiously fluted. The rod was held horizontal some inches from the floor by a weight of some sort at one end and a contraption of wire and parchment at the other. As soon as his hands had explored this wire framework Toby realized that what had tripped him was an overturned standard lamp.

His hands also told him that the bulb of the lamp had been shattered.

Getting to his feet, he started a slow progress round the room, running his hand along the wall, in search of a door and the probable light switch beside it. On his way he encountered other pieces of overturned furniture, first a chair, then a table, then a reading lamp. Then he trod on something that crunched under his shoe, something that seemed to be the remnants of a china figure; as he bent down to feel it he could trace the shape of head and shoulders and the smooth, cold features of the molded face. At last he found the light switch. Pressing it, he stood blinking dazzled eyes at the room as lights leaped up inside a great glass bowl against the ceiling.

For an instant he stood perfectly still. Then slowly his hand fell back to his side. He thrust the hand into a pocket and brought out a packet of cigarettes. Without shifting his gaze from the far end of the room, he stuck a cigarette between his lips, lit it, and breathed the smoke in deeply.

The room was high and long, with furniture of the glass-and-chromium kind and a carpet of deep purple. The white walls were stippled with silver, with mirrors let into them here and there in narrow panels. The curtains were of purple and silver brocade; there were quantities of white chrysanthemums in silver bowls; there were several huge ash trays of thick purple glass; there was a long, low bookcase that stretched the whole length of one wall, and at the far end of the room there was a writing table, an enormous piece of furniture in polished black.

But from end to end of this dream out of Hollywood havoc had swept. The chrysanthemums lay trampled on the floor, with the water from their bowls making dark patches on the carpet; chairs and little tables lay scattered or broken, and ash and cigarette stubs from the purple ash trays smeared the carpet with flaky gray. One of the panels of looking glass had been smashed. The face of the glazed figure on which Toby had trodden looked up at him blankly from a point near the bookcase, while the legs and feet lay near the middle of the room.

But besides all these signs of a wild struggle there were signs of another kind of violence.

Where shards of mirror had fallen away from the broken panel two small holes pitted the wall behind. On the floor, in a line between the mirror and the desk, was a stain that was darker and stickier looking than those made by the water from the spilled flower bowls. On the desk, next to a chromium inkstand, lay a revolver.

Yet it was not at the revolver, lying on a square of blotting paper, that Toby was staring as he stood by the door, smoke trickling slowly through his lips. He was staring at the man who sat at the desk.

In the midst of the scene of havoc, with hands placidly folded, eyes closed, and lips mildly smiling, the man whom Toby Dyke had come to see was very peacefully dead.

2

TOBY DYKE WALKED FORWARD. He stood still, facing the
dead man across the desk. He took long puffs at his cigarette. For at least a minute he stood there before he
touched anything.

The man in the chair was about thirty-six years old.
He was on the short side and plumpish, with a plump
face that in life had been florid and animated. Sandy hair
grew scantily above a rounded brow. As Toby remembered him, there had always been a sort of evasive affability about him which even in death had not quite vanished. He was wearing a dinner jacket. His shirt front
was uncrumpled and his tie was straight; there was no
sign that he had suffered violence.

Toby took an empty matchbox out of his pocket and
knocked the ash from his cigarette into the box. His gaze

was hard and puzzled. Glancing round the room again, he stared at the stain of blood on the floor. Though it was small, it was heavily clotted, as if the blood had flowed there for some minutes. Looking back at the revolver, Toby picked it up carefully and saw that three shots had been fired from it.

Bleakly frowning, he studied the dead man. Toby had seen John Lestarke-Toye only once during the year that had passed since John's marriage to Lili Dános. That had been in London, six months ago. . . . With a slight jerk of the shoulders Toby seemed suddenly to become aware of the wireless set talking on and on. Striding across to it, he switched it off. Then he walked round the desk and bent over the dead man, straightening again after a moment, mangling his cigarette between taut lips. It had been only a few weeks after Constance Crane had left for America that John had married Lili Dános. Now Constance was still in America, and John was dead, and Lili was—where? Toby's gaze, bright with uneasy questions, went back to the sticky stain on the carpet.

After another moment he crossed to the door and opened it. He shouted. Dimly the echoes of his own voice answered him. He turned back into the room. Closing the door, he returned to the desk and picked up a telephone pad he had noticed. Flicking over the pages, he found what he was looking for. "Dr. Gayson—Mallowby 51." With his hand wrapped in a handkerchief he picked up the telephone on the desk and asked for the doctor's number.

When the doctor replied Toby began crisply: "I'm

speaking from Redvers, the home of Mr. Toye. I believe you're Mr. Toye's usual medical attendant?"

"Yes," came the answer. "That's to say—you're speaking of Mr. Lestarke-Toye?"

"Sorry," said Toby, "I generally forget the Lestarke; he didn't bother with it until he got married. Can you get over here straight away, Dr. Gayson? Mr. Lestarke-Toye is dead."

He heard the doctor's exclamation. Then came a sharp question: "Who is it speaking?"

"I'm a friend of Mr. Lestarke-Toye's," said Toby.

"Ah. Then please tell Mrs. Lestarke-Toye I'll be with her as quickly as I can."

"She isn't here," said Toby.

"She isn't?"

"No. In fact, I appear to be the only person in the house."

"Dear me, how very unfortunate. Oh, but surely you don't mean the servants aren't there?"

"It appears to be a servantless house."

"How strange, how very strange," said the doctor. "Well, I can't be with you in less than a quarter of an hour, but I'll come as quickly as I can. I'm very sorry indeed to hear of Mr. Lestarke-Toye's death. I warned him, of course, but I'm sorry, very sorry . . ." There was a click as the doctor rang off.

Toby, with another look at the man who was sitting there in the indifferent calm of death amid the wreckage of a room that had bullets in the wall and blood on the floor, murmured: "So he warned you, did he? But I wonder if he really warned you of—this."

Returning to the door, tossing the stub of his cigarette into the fireplace as he passed it, he walked out into the darkness and silence of the empty house.

He turned on lights as he came to them.

The house had been built in the worst taste of the end of the nineteenth century and had been modernized in the worst taste of the twentieth. Through hall and passages purple and silver still predominated. Smooth walls sprouted suddenly into clusters of floral molding; the furniture, except in the aggressively Tudor dining room and among the hectic frills and laces of Lili's bedroom, was glassily bleak. There were not really many rooms, though at least on the ground floor they were spacious. The bedrooms were smaller, particularly the servants' rooms on the top floor, which were poked away under the curious slopes and angles of the gables. Toby spent some minutes going through these attics. There were used sheets on the beds and soap and towels on the washstands, but all drawers were empty and there were no signs, either in cupboards or under the beds, of the hampers and cheap suitcases that make up a maidservant's luggage. As he went down to the next floor again Toby's long, sallow face was grimly thoughtful.

He looked into Lili's bedroom and into the green sea cave of her perfumed bathroom. As with Lili herself, there was a stereotyped extravagance about both rooms. The array of coats and gowns that hung in her dress cupboards made it impossible to guess whether she had left the house with luggage or without it, and a quick survey of her cosmetics told as little, for again her supplies were so abundant as to reveal nothing. Toby went on into John's bedroom.

It was the most rational room in the house, but in a strange disorder. John's tweeds had been thrown down on the bed; some socks were on the floor; a drawer was half open with ties and collars hanging out of it. In John's bathroom Toby found water in the bath, but the water was clear as if it had not been used, and the cake of soap in the small niche in the wall above the bath was dry. Standing for a minute or two staring at the clear water, Toby rather absently stooped and dabbled a hand in it. The water was quite cold. Drying his hand on his handkerchief, he went on to look at the other bedrooms.

All three looked as if they had been prepared for visitors. There was fresh linen on the beds and a vase of fresh flowers in each room. But in one room only there were signs of occupation. A suitcase had been opened; though, except for a few toilet things, it had not been unpacked. It looked as if the visitor had only troubled to tidy himself hurriedly on arrival. He seemed to have had time, however, to smoke a cigarette, for there was its stub in an ash tray, and on the floor, in front of the electric heater, was the spill with which the cigarette had presumably been lit.

Toby went swiftly through the things in the suitcase. They were cheap, shabby, and had been carelessly packed. He found a shirt with the initials J. P. U. in marking ink on the collarband and a book that had the name J. Porter Ugbrook scrawled in pencil on the fly-leaf. As he read the name Toby's black eyebrows went up and his lips rounded in a soft whistle.

He had just replaced the things in the suitcase when he heard the doctor's ring. He hurried downstairs to answer it.

But halfway down the stairs Toby wheeled suddenly, went leaping up them again, returned to J. Porter Ugbrook's room, crossed to the fireplace, picked up the half-burned spill, untwisted it, and scanned what was written on the paper.

Under the charred marks at the top the few sentences ran:

. . . and so I shall rely on you to come to my help, because I must have help from someone I can trust. No one in the past has given me the sort of help and sympathy I have had again and again from you. Perhaps you are kind and wise enough to be able to take this last demand on you as a form of gratitude. But in any case—come. Telephone if you can and let me know when to meet you.

Yours ever,

JOHN

As the doctor's third impatient ring sounded through the house Toby quickly pressed the piece of paper back into the folds it had had when he found it and dropped it back onto the hearth.

Toby Dyke found Dr. Gayson on the doorstep, huddled inside a dark overcoat. Aged about fifty, the doctor was a slight, brisk man with a cold manner and a look of some intelligence.

"Except that we're not as at sea as I feel, Dr. Gayson," said Toby, "you could take this house for the *Marie Celeste*."

The doctor stepped inside and peeled off his gloves.

"You mean there's really no one here?"

"Not a living soul."

"Then in that case would it be impertinent to ask just who you are and how you got here?" The doctor looked Toby up and down. "I don't think I've ever seen you before."

"My name's Dyke, and I'm an old friend of John Toye's," said Toby. "I came here because I was invited, though from the look of things, I should say I missed the best of the party."

"And was there nobody, no servant or anyone, to answer the door when you got here?" asked Gayson.

"I've told you, nobody," said Toby.

"Then how did you get in?"

"By the french windows at the back of the house."

"You mean you forced a way in?"

Toby swung round on the doctor. He said: "Listen, suspicion at times has its function, but in a house as full as this is of things that stink with suspiciousness, don't waste too much of your mental energy on me. As a matter of fact, the french windows were unfastened, but if they hadn't been I should have forced my way in. I didn't like the look of things."

"I am not suspicious," said the doctor gravely. "I

merely want to get things as straight as I can. It all seems to me very curious—all except the death of Mr. Lestarke-Toye. That, I'm afraid, I was expecting."

"But not like this you weren't." Toby thrust the door open.

The doctor went a few steps into the room. At the change in his face Toby gave a sour sort of smile. Gayson stood still, and after his first look at the dead man seated at the desk his startled gaze went slowly round the room.

"You're quite right . . . I wasn't expecting this." Shocked, bewildered, his eyes dropped to the stain of blood on the floor.

"I haven't called the police yet," said Toby. "I was leaving that to you."

"It's queer," muttered Gayson. "It's . . . I don't understand it at all. What's happened to Mrs. Lestarke-Toye and the servants?"

"And what's happened to Mr. J. Porter Ugbrook," asked Toby, "who appears to have vanished like the dew with the rest of them?"

"Ugbrook?" said the doctor uncertainly. "That's a name I seem to know."

"He's a writer whom the firm of Banner and Crane have been boosting rather hard lately; you've probably seen the advertisements. There's a suitcase of his in a room upstairs."

"Ah yes, Banner and Crane . . . They're the publishers Mr. Lestarke-Toye's associated with, aren't they?" Gayson crossed the room. He bent over the still form of John Lestarke-Toye. Toby stood watching in silence. Presently Gayson said, glancing up: "You know, Mr. Dyke, this death *is* exactly as I expected it. Sudden, peaceful . . . I expect you know his heart's been rotten for years. And lately, well, I warned him."

"So he was expecting to die?"

"Poor devil, yes." Standing upright again, Gayson put out a hand toward the revolver.

Toby intervened: "I shouldn't touch that. But if you're interested, three shots have been fired from it, and there are only two in the wall."

"And everything was just like this when you arrived?"

"Except that the wireless was on." Toby sat down on the edge of a low couch. "Oh—and the light wasn't. . . . Have you any idea how long ago he died?"

"At a guess, something like three hours—but that's only a guess."

"That means round about six o'clock. Six o'clock . . . There's something very wrong indeed about all this. You're dead sure . . . you're dead sure that Toye died a natural death?"

"How could I be sure?" asked Gayson. "I've told you I was expecting him to go and to go just like that. I'd told him any unusual exertion might be the end of him. There's nothing at all about the body that's inconsistent with his condition, and if I'd been called to this house by a frantic Mrs. Lestarke-Toye and found it full of excited servants and this room as tidy as I've always seen it, and found Lestarke-Toye himself sitting at his desk just like that, then I'd say yes, I was sure he'd died a natural death, and I should unhesitatingly have signed a certificate. But as it is . . ."

"You'll want an inquest?"

Gayson nodded.

"Good," said Toby.

As Gayson looked at him curiously Toby crossed the room again, once more draped his handkerchief over the telephone, and picked it up. He held it toward the doctor. "If you don't mind . . . the police."

"You know, Mr. Dyke," said the doctor, hesitating before taking the telephone, "it seems to me you don't act quite as most people would, or at any rate as I should expect them to act, on the scene of—well, a scene like this."

"That's because, in a sense, scenes like this are my job. And that, I'm inclined to think now, may be the explanation of why I was invited. I haven't been invited before. Mrs. Lestarke-Toye didn't like her husband's friends."

"I see," said Gayson doubtfully. He took the telephone, but slowly he put it down on its stand again.

"I was just wondering . . . I was just wondering about Mrs. Lestarke-Toye," he said. "I've got an idea where she might have gone."

"Then suppose you fetch her."

"I'm not at all certain about it," said the doctor, "and if I was wrong it might be very awkward, but I could telephone and find out if she's there."

"Go ahead then," said Toby.

"Before I call the police?"

"She might be grateful."

Hesitantly Gayson picked up the telephone again.

As he asked for a number Toby seated himself on a chair close to the remains of the fire and held his hands out over the embers. Stooping over them, his eyes reflected their reddish glow. He heard the doctor ask for Sir Wilfred Ridden. A moment later the doctor was asking Sir Wilfred Ridden whether Mrs. Lestarke-Toye happened to be with him. There was a staccato uneasiness in Gayson's tone which his attempt at speaking casually did not conceal. By mistake he even went on sounding casual when he was explaining into the telephone that Mrs. Lestarke-Toye's husband had been found dead. Toby's lower lip protruded in sardonic comment, and he waited to have the local scandal explained to him.

But Gayson, replacing the telephone, only shook his head. "She isn't there."

"And isn't there anyone else she might be visiting?" asked Toby.

"I don't know—and now Ridden knows about it and says he's coming over; I'm sorry about that."

"Why?"

"Well, I imagine the police won't want to find a flock of people here, will they?"

"A flock of witnesses wouldn't be bad."

Gayson grunted. He telephoned again, this time to the police station.

When the doctor had given his message Toby asked him: "Who is this man Ridden?"

"A friend of the Lestarke-Toyes'. His place is only a short walk away through the woods. Can't you suggest somewhere Mrs. Lestarke-Toye might have gone, Mr. Dyke?"

"I'm sorry, I know next to nothing about her," said Toby.

"She's Hungarian, isn't she?"

"I believe so. Her name was Dános before her first marriage, and she went back to using that name after her first husband died. I imagine she thought it wouldn't have helped her on the screen to be known as Mrs. Snape."

"I expect she was right." Gayson laughed shortly. "But she dropped her career when she married, didn't she? Rather a pity in a way. With looks like that she ought to have been a success."

"All the looks in the world won't always help if you haven't the first rudiments of a knowledge of how to act," said Toby. "Fortunately for her, by the time she'd found that out she'd got a rich husband."

"You sound somewhat prejudiced against her," said Gayson, watching him.

"Sorry," said Toby. Knocking ash off his cigarette, he glowered at the fire.

"And you think," said Gayson after a moment, "that what Lestarke-Toye wanted you for may have been something to do with whatever it was that happened here this evening?"

"As you say, it may have been."

"I always liked Lestarke-Toye," said Gayson slowly.

"He seemed to me a very decent sort of chap. I'm sorry things have happened like this. There's bound to be a good deal of trouble, and besides——" He broke off, listening.

Toby, too, had heard a noise.

It was the noise of a car, and it sounded nearer than the road. It came closer, as if it had just taken the bend in the drive, then a moment later it stopped.

Toby looked up at Gayson. "That's quick for the police."

"It's probably Ridden," said Gayson. "I thought he'd walk over, but perhaps the cold made him decide to come by car."

"Sh!" said Toby sharply.

The front door had opened. They heard the click of the latch as it closed again, but as the deep carpet in the hall would deaden any sound of footsteps they could not be certain for an instant whether or not anyone had entered. But the next moment a voice was suddenly raised. It was a woman's voice, singing. The words of the song fell on the ears of the two startled men with a sweet, ringing richness.

> *"Oh, what care I for my house and land?*
> *Oh, what care I for my money-o?*
> *Oh, what care I for my new-wedded lord?*
> *I'm off with the raggle-taggle gypsies-o!"*

"My God," exclaimed Gayson, starting across the room, "it's Mrs. Lestarke-Toye, and she's going to walk in here and——"

Before he reached it the door opened.

At sight of the woman who stood there, her song bitten off and her whole body jerking back as her gaze swept down the room to dwell in horror-filled brilliance on the quiet man who sat at the desk, Toby leaped to his feet.

One word came from him in a harsh exclamation: "Constance!"

3

CONSTANCE CRANE came into the room.

Daughter of Norman Crane, who with the money of old Simon Banner had made the firm of Banner and Crane, she was a slender, cool, composed woman, the kind whose appearance scarcely changes between the ages of thirty and forty. She had a small, pale face and large eyes under clearly marked, arched eyebrows, fair hair waving crisply back from a low forehead, a lithe, upright carriage, and very good ankles. She was wearing a small hat of light green felt and a dark fur coat which she held tightly around her. Since her father's death five years before she had been head of the firm of Banner and Crane. John Lestarke-Toye had been her partner.

She came only a few steps into the room, then stood still. She was breathing deeply and jerkily.

Toby went toward her. He slipped a hand under her arm.

In a voice that had had all expression shocked out of it she said dully: "Hullo, Toby."

But she was looking past him. When she had spoken her lips remained parted a little. Toby could feel how her arm was trembling.

After a moment he said softly: "Come, Constance— let's go into one of the other rooms."

She did not move.

He began again: "Constance . . ."

He saw a slight twitch of her features. It was not the beginning of tears, but some kind of nervous contraction.

"He *is* dead, isn't he?" she asked huskily.

"I'm afraid so," said Toby.

"When did it happen?"

"Dr. Gayson thinks around six o'clock."

She glanced toward the doctor as if she had only just realized his presence. Toby introduced them.

"It's his heart, I suppose?" she said.

Gayson replied: "Probably."

"It must be his heart. His heart was always bad." She began to draw off her gloves. Her fur coat, swinging open, revealed the light green tailored suit she was wearing. "Poor John. D'you know . . . ?" She hesitated, and her voice dropped to a whisper. "He looks as if he almost *enjoys* being dead!"

"That's better than if he looked the other way, isn't it?" said Toby.

Her eyes met his for an instant. "You always did take

death rather laconically, Toby. I suppose that's fortunate —for all of us—at the moment. How did all this . . . ?" She gestured at the overturned furniture and the smashed mirror, then let the hand she had gestured with fall to her side. She stood staring at the clotted blood on the carpet. "How did all this happen?"

"We don't know," said Toby.

"You weren't here when it happened?"

"No."

"And you know nothing about it?"

"Nothing whatever."

She let out a jerky breath. Turning, she made her way to a chair. She walked in the heavy, uncertain fashion of a person suffering from shock, and as she dropped into the chair she wrapped her coat around her again and shivered.

Toby said, looking down at her: "The police are coming. Now suppose we go through to one of the other rooms, Constance. There's no need for us to stay in here. We could go into one of the other rooms and get a fire going. And perhaps we can hunt out a drink from somewhere."

But again she was looking toward the desk.

"The drink wouldn't be a bad idea," she said absently, "and if you've a cigarette . . ." She tugged off her hat and pressed a hand against her forehead. "I left my cigarettes in the car or somewhere . . . I don't remember. Toby"—her voice sharpened suddenly—"where's Lili?"

"That's another thing we don't know."

"Isn't that rather upsetting in view of . . . ?" She pointed listlessly at the havoc.

"Yes," said Toby, holding out a packet of cigarettes to her, "as you say—upsetting."

"At any rate," she said, "I'm glad you're here. Though I'm almost as surprised at finding you here as myself. What brought you?"

"An invitation," said Toby. "What brought you?"

Again he saw that slight twitch of her features.

As she did not reply he went on: "I thought you were still in America."

"Did you?" she said vaguely.

"How long have you been back?"

"A week."

"Why didn't you let me know?"

"Ought I to have? I didn't think of it. When I got back I felt rather as if there was no one . . ." She looked down at the fire, then up at him, waiting for a light.

Toby groped for his matches. "Well, what brought you back from America, Constance?"

"Aren't you asking an awful lot of questions?" she asked.

"Do you mind?"

"At the moment . . . yes."

She bent her head over the flame.

A startled gleam came into Toby's eyes and the hand that held the match went rigid. For as Constance Crane raised the cigarette to her lips, holding it there with two fingers as she thrust its tip into the flame, Toby saw that round and under the nail of one of the fingers there was a dry, brown stain.

As she raised her eyes Toby swiftly raised his so that she should not notice that he had been staring.

"Thanks," said Constance, either for the cigarette or for the fact that his questions had stopped. She leaned back in her chair. Her voice sounded more even, but her cheeks were grayish under her light make-up. "I'll talk as much as you like presently. I'll be glad to talk to you, Toby. I seem to have had no one to talk to properly for ages. But just at the moment I can't feel and I can't think. . . . It was a terrible shock, walking in here. But I don't want to break down; that won't help anyone."

With his gaze on the thin line of brown running round her nail, Toby commented dryly: "I think you're keeping your head pretty well in the circumstances, Constance."

Behind them Dr. Gayson cleared his throat. Strolling forward, he stood looking down at Constance. He said: "I was just wondering, Miss Crane, how did you get in?"

"In where?" she asked.

"Into the house."

"By the front door. Didn't you hear me?"

"Yes, I know you came in by the front door," said Gayson. "But I meant, how? Was the door open?"

"Not open. It was closed. But it wasn't locked."

Toby said: "I expect we didn't shut it properly after you arrived."

"Quite so," said Gayson. "But you mean, Miss Crane,

you usually walk into houses like that without ringing first and announce your presence by singing?"

She looked at him for a moment before replying. "Suppose I do?"

"I can scarcely believe it."

"Then, like the White Queen, you should practice believing!"

As Gayson frowned Toby said: "Miss Crane has just said she doesn't feel fit to talk just at present."

But Constance herself went on: "You see, Dr. Gayson, for several years I used to have a key of John's flat and he used to have one of mine." There were touches of color in her cheeks; her tone had a high, false flippancy. "We weren't accustomed to ringing when we visited one another."

"Constance, there's no need for you to answer anyone's questions," Toby warned her sharply.

"I know that," she said indifferently. "But I don't mind what questions I answer, except that——" She snapped the sentence off short. Jerking upright in her chair, sitting tautly like that for a moment, she said in a harsh whisper: "There's someone outside."

"I didn't hear anything," said Toby.

"Ssh!" she said.

They listened.

"There," she said, looking from one to the other, "didn't you hear it?"

"It must be Ridden," said the doctor. "He usually comes that way through the wood. I'm sorry my telephoning has landed him on our hands. He's a good fellow in his way, but not always tactful or helpful." He crossed to the window.

Toby noticed that as the doctor drew aside the purple and silver curtains Constance was watching with a tense air of strain, crushing the end of her cigarette between her rigid fingers.

Toby said again: "I didn't hear anything."

She shot a glance at him. "I heard footsteps and a queer sound like a—a sort of *plop!*"

The doctor pushed open the french windows. He peered into the darkness.

"Hullo!" he called. "Hullo—Ridden!" After an instant he looked round at them. "It can't be Ridden. Are you sure you heard something, Miss Crane?"

"Didn't you?" she asked.

"I wasn't listening for anything." Gayson started to close the doors again. "Anyway, I don't think there's anyone there now."

But Constance, springing swiftly to her feet, ran across the room and thrust past him into the dark garden.

"There was—I *know* there was something," she said desperately. Standing with her coat clutched around her and the light from the open window falling on her face, she said again: "I *know* there was something!"

Toby said quietly: "Well, does it matter such a lot if there was?"

"But that sound I heard . . ." There was an agony of terror in her voice that sounded very strange, coming from Constance Crane.

"All right," said Gayson, evidently catching that note

in her voice too, "we'll take a look if you like. However, I don't expect we'll find——"

"Look!" she cried, and a thin finger shot out, pointing. "Look—over there by the trees! I saw something move. Please, Toby, go and look!"

Gayson had already started across the lawn.

"But what about leaving you here alone?" asked Toby dubiously.

"I'm all right. But please—look carefully!"

He looked into her face, then said: "All right, Constance." As she turned to go back into the lighted room he set off in the same direction as the doctor.

The darkness ahead was intense. When Toby had gone only a few yards the light from the windows behind was cut off by Constance closing the doors and drawing the curtains. Grinning, Toby stood still. The grin gave a rather wolfish expression to his sallow face. As soon as he judged Gayson must have reached the trees at the far side of the lawn he turned, went straight back to the house, and silently edged the french windows open.

Constance had carelessly left a chink between the curtains, and Toby, without touching them, was able to see into the room. At what he saw, one of his black eyebrows shot up.

With no trace of her recent terror about her, though patches of bright, nervous red flamed in her cheeks, Constance Crane was bending over the body of John Lestarke-Toye, and her hands, competently, ruthlessly, were searching through each of his pockets in turn.

As Toby stepped into the room she sprang backward with a cry.

"You unspeakable, bloody fool, Constance!" Toby spoke through set teeth.

She said: "I—I was just looking for something."

"Come away from there," he ordered sharply. "It's lucky it was I and not Gayson who had the idea of coming back to see why you were so keen to get rid of us. Are you trying to get yourself in a mess on purpose?"

The red died out of her cheeks. She said: "Yes . . . it's true I wanted to get rid of you. But that was only because I wanted to—to be alone with John for a minute. You don't seem to remember"—her voice cracked suddenly as if tears were coming—"I used to be in love with him once."

"And so the only way you could think of spending the minute you had alone with him was to go through his pockets. Well, well. What were you looking for?"

"For nothing—for nothing that matters to anyone but myself."

"Not even to the police?"

"Of course not to the police."

"Stop being a fool, Constance."

"Then stop asking questions you've no right to ask. You said yourself just now that I don't have to answer anyone's questions if I don't want to."

He walked across to the fireplace. He cursed down at the dead embers for a moment, then fell silent.

After an instant Constance came to his side. He felt her hand on his arm.

"I'm sorry, Toby. I know I've been stupid, and I know you only want to help me. You've always been an awfully good friend. But when you walked in just now I felt startled and frightened. This whole thing's so terrible. . . . I'm sorry I spoke like that."

Without looking round he put a hand over hers and pressed it.

"I don't really mind telling you what I was looking for," she went on, "because I think you'll understand. But as a matter of fact, the idea came to me as an after-thought when I thought I was alone with John. You see, I suddenly started wondering whether he'd kept about him any of the things I gave him. For instance, there was a watch with some words engraved on it. And there was . . . Oh well, it doesn't matter, but there were all sorts of things that I shouldn't like the police to paw over, getting their horrid minds to work on John and me. I know it was stupid of me, but—you do under-stand, don't you, Toby?"

"I think so," he replied, "and you're quite right—you were very stupid. You were very stupid indeed to think that after a year of marriage to as jealous a wife as Lili, John might still be carrying around with him any mementos of you. In fact, it was so very stupid, Con-stance, that I still want to know what you were really looking for. And just between you and me, Constance . . ." Her grip on his sleeve had grown firmer; as he spoke he lifted her hand off his sleeve, and as she tried violently to jerk it away from him he opened out the fingers so that the light fell on the brown stain that edged one nail.

"Just between you and me, Constance," said Toby as they looked at one another, "what did you find *the first time* you arrived here this evening?"

4

As she edged away from him Toby went on: "I don't know what time you got here, whether it was before or after John's death; I don't know whether the shock you acted when you came in was genuine or not. But I do know that if you'd only just arrived, expecting to find both Lili and the normal complement of servants in the house, you'd never have walked in as if you owned the place and then burst into song. I didn't want to encourage that doctor in his suspicions, but he was perfectly right—it isn't your normal way of entering a house. And this is blood on your nail, Constance. Well"—as he let her hand go—"what about it?"

But her eyelids were lowered and her face said nothing. Only when he urged her again she started speaking in a cold, angry voice: "I'm afraid even you sometimes make mistakes, Toby. This isn't blood on my nail. As a matter of fact, I did my nails with a rather dark-colored varnish this morning, and then I remembered that John always hated painted nails, so I wiped the varnish off. But I was in rather a hurry, so I suppose I didn't do it properly. And about my singing—yes, I admit it wasn't normal. But I was feeling so queer about seeing John again that I think it was sheer nerves made me act as I did."

"I believe you," said Toby. "I'm sure it was sheer nerves that made you sing—but not on account of seeing John again. You'd already seen him. It was those two cars out there—the doctor's and mine—the fact that other people had turned up, that got you jittery."

"Oh, believe what you like," she said. "But it's a pity you're insisting on getting things twisted up. It isn't going to help."

"Listen," he said, "why don't you tell me what you were doing here earlier?"

"I wasn't here earlier."

"All right," he said, "you weren't. We'll stick to that if you insist. I hope you'll be able to back it with an alibi when the police start questioning you—and to give a reasonable explanation of what you're doing here."

"I can show them the invitation John sent me," she said. "And I can tell them what made me accept it. You seem to be forgetting, Toby, that John and I are—were—partners in business. And when I got a cable from Mark Fenning—he's in charge of the accounts department now —which suggested that John had gone quite off his head,

I thought I'd better come back from New York. I've talked to Mark, and I've been investigating one or two things, and what I've discovered certainly makes it look as if John had gone mad. I was going to get in touch with John and insist on an explanation when I got his invitation. I don't know whether the reason he asked me down here was anything to do with this—this queer thing I've been telling you about, or whether it was just that he wanted to see me again. Anyway, I'd got to see him, so I came."

"I suppose you don't want to tell me what you mean when you say that John had gone mad?" said Toby.

"I don't in the least mind telling you," she replied. "It's to do with a man called J. Porter Ugbrook——" She stopped. Outside the window there was a sound of footsteps. As the glass doors opened Toby caught her quick whisper: "I'll tell you later."

Dr. Gayson was not alone. With him was a tall man in tweeds, who was aged about forty, with eyes of an uncommonly pale blue and bristling eyebrows like gilded antennae. His skin was reddish and freckled; he had big red hands and wrists. As he stepped into the room and stood blinking in the light Gayson introduced the newcomer as Sir Wilfred Ridden.

Rubbing chilled hands together, Gayson went on: "I feel sure you were mistaken, Miss Crane, in thinking there was anyone wandering round the garden. I've looked very carefully indeed. There are no traces of anyone, and I heard nothing whatever until I heard Sir Wilfred walking up through the wood."

"I must have made a mistake," said Constance, managing an apologetic smile. "But thank you very much for looking. It's the shock, I'm afraid, made me imagine things."

Sir Wilfred Ridden, who had stopped blinking and had raised one of his big red hands in an incongruously breezy greeting to Constance and Toby, turned toward the dead man.

Ridden's voice was powerful but wheezy, like a gust of the north wind blowing. "Poor fellow," he said with a whistling blast of pity, "poor, poor fellow. My God, makes you think, doesn't it? I always say there's nothing like sudden death for making you think."

"Pity, then, there isn't more of it in some circles," said Toby.

He noticed that Constance had thrust her hands, with the telltale stain on one of them, deep into the pockets of her coat. She seemed to have lost her nervousness and to be merely pallidly, wearily thoughtful. Dr. Gayson also looked as if he were thinking hard.

Ridden eyed Toby doubtfully, then went on in a worried tone: "Jove, it does shake you up, though, when you see a chap sitting there dead when you were talking to him only a few hours ago." He glanced at his watch. "Matter of fact, it wasn't much over four hours. What a rum business life is, isn't it? I think it was round about half-past five we met. We stood and chatted for a few minutes. Jove, if only I'd known . . . Don't mean I could've done anything about his heart, poor old fellow; still, if one had known he'd only got half an hour or so to live, one wouldn't just have said, 'Oh, hullo,' and 'Cold evening,' and all that sort of thing; I mean, one'd have tried to say something more suitable. And one wouldn't have let him go off home by himself. Jove, I feel sorry! But I didn't realize . . . That was the trouble, you see, I didn't realize."

"Where John Lestarke-Toye is now," said Toby, "I feel sure you are forgiven. Where did you say you met him, Sir Wilfred?"

"Down by old Hogben's cottage. I'd just been in to see Hogben about his roof, and there was old John just going by, so I called out and said, 'Hullo,' and he said, 'Hullo,' and we talked for a couple of minutes, and then I said, 'Coming my way?' and he said, 'No, I think I'll go this way,' and then I said, 'So long,' and he said, 'So long,' and then he went off home up the hill and I went off home the other way. But I tell you, if I'd known . . ."

Toby turned to Gayson. "Whereabouts is Hogben's cottage?"

"Down at the bottom of Hanger Hill," said Gayson. "You must have come up Hanger Hill yourself if you came from London. It's the very steep hill just before you get here."

"A white cottage with another road branching off beside it?"

"That's it."

"But look here," said Ridden, looking around him as if he had only just begun to take in the disorder of the room, "look here—all this mess here—what the devil does it mean? Extraordinary business—I mean old John getting mixed up in a roughhouse like this. Not his style at all. Peaceable chap if ever there was one. I wish somebody'd tell me what happened."

"So do the rest of us," said Toby.

"You don't any of you know? Jove," said Ridden, "what an extraordinary business. I'll tell you what I think must've happened. I think old John got into a scrap with somebody and that was what made his heart pop off. Poor old fellow." But as he added thoughtfully: "Some scrap!" it sounded as if he were rather envious.

"As you say," said Toby, "some scrap."

"For heaven's sake!" exclaimed Constance.

As they looked at her she went on tensely: "For heaven's sake, don't stand there talking in that inane fashion when we ought to be trying to get in touch with Lili. Lili's John's wife and John's dead. D'you want her to have to find that out from the papers?"

"But we don't know where she is," said Toby.

"Can't you ring up some of her friends and try to find out?"

"Who are her friends?" he asked.

"Oh . . . oh, but there must be something we can do to find her. I know!" She went toward the desk. "Try ringing up some of the numbers on this telephone pad."

"An excellent idea," said Gayson.

As Toby picked up the pad and once more flicked over the pages Gayson went on: "The police ought to arrive any moment now. You know, I'm almost more worried by the absence of all the servants than by the absence of Mrs. Lestarke-Toye. She may be away on a visit; she may even have gone to the cinema. But why should all the servants have cleared out? Did something happen here to frighten them, and if so, why haven't any of them reported it?"

Toby, frowning at the list of names and numbers, said: "I don't know where to begin. There are too many people down here."

Constance snatched the pad away. "Oh, try any of them. Look—here's Mrs. Werth. Try her. She's a great friend of Lili's. It was Mrs. Werth who introduced Lili to John, and I imagine she's kept a finger in Lili's life ever since. Here—Museum 77192. Go on, Toby."

Shrugging, he picked up the telephone. After a little he said: "I don't think there's anyone in. I can hear it ringing. What number shall I try next?"

"Give it a moment more," said Constance.

He gave it a moment, then repeated: "Whom shall I try next?"

But it was just then, as he was removing the telephone from his ear, that the ringing sound stopped and a reedy voice gasped a breathless "Hullo."

"Hullo," said Toby, "is that Mrs. Werth?"

"No, it isn't," said the voice, "it's Billy Werth, and it's really very awkward anyone ringing up just at the moment, unless it's very important, because there's no one at home but me and I'm not very well. I got out of bed specially to answer the telephone. But if it's Mother you want, she's out, so if you'll just ring up again presently——"

"Hi, wait a moment, Billy! This is Toby Dyke speaking."

"Oh, hullo, Toby. I'm sorry Mother isn't in. She's gone to a concert. And I really mustn't stand here, because I'm all upset inside and——"

"Wait a moment, Billy. Is your sister in?"

"No, Leora's out too. She's always out. She's taken up slumming. Really, Toby, I ought to go back to bed and——"

"For the Lord's sake, will you hold on a moment, Billy!" Toby's hand tightened on the telephone. "It's something very important. Is Lili Lestarke-Toye there?"

"No, why should she be?" asked Billy.

"We're trying to find her. It's very important."

"Well, I'm awfully sorry, Toby, I don't know anything about her. I've been in bed all day. It's my stomach, you know; I'm feeling really dreadful. And this hall's so drafty, I really don't think I ought to stand here any longer."

"All right, run along, Billy, run along. But listen," said Toby, "will you remember to ask your mother when she comes in whether or not she's seen anything of Lili? If she has, ask her to ring me up at Redvers. It's very important."

"Very well. But you know my stomach gets upset so easily, Toby. I think it's a sort of chill I've got really, though Mother says I ate too many mince pies."

"All right, Billy, run along. I'm sorry you aren't well." Toby put the telephone down.

He turned round to ask Constance what number to try next.

But she was no longer at his elbow. Gayson was still standing near the desk, and Ridden was straddling the cold hearth. But though while he had been telephoning Toby had heard no sound—no footsteps, no opening and shutting of doors—Constance had gone.

Cursing at the other two men for not having stopped her, Toby strode across the room and out into the hall. At the other end of the hall the front door was gaping, showing him an oblong of darkness and of starry sky.

5

TOBY GLANCED BACK over his shoulder at the room where Ridden and Gayson had started talking, then he walked quietly across the hall.

In the light from the open doorway he saw that Constance's car was still in the drive, drawn up behind his own at the foot of the steps. He laughed and, propping one shoulder against a doorpost, he waited.

With one ear he listened to the sound of voices in the room, and with the other for any sound that might come from the dark garden. But the garden, in the hard, cold grip of the frost, was silent. Now and then cars went by on the highroad, their headlights sending up an amber glow above the hedges and their engines throbbing as they toiled up the hill. Toby's lips parted to emit the faint, hissing sound of a smothered whistle. Thoughts hurried behind the brooding look in his eyes. The chill of the air felt almost like something solid pressing against his face.

At the very moment when Toby heard the tap of light footsteps on the gravel he saw headlights swing in at the gate. Out of the darkness Constance came and stood at his side.

"I've been down to the garage," she said softly. "There's nothing in it."

"We can't talk now," he replied. "Here are the police."

"I don't want to talk. I'm just telling you—there isn't any car in the garage."

"All right, then, there isn't. What does it matter?"

The headlights were following the sweep of the drive up to the house. She asked: "Isn't it important whether or not Lili went away in the car?"

"How d'you know it was Lili who went away in it? It may have been any of the servants, or J. Porter Ugbrook."

"But——"

"I told you we can't talk now," he said. "But listen— we'd better talk later. Meanwhile keep your head, and if you want to stick to that story that you weren't here earlier in the evening, make sure it's watertight."

"But I wasn't here earlier!"

"Ssh! . . ."

They were standing in silence, side by side in the doorway, when the police car drew up at the foot of the steps.

An inspector, a sergeant, and two constables got out of the car. Dr. Gayson came out to meet them.

With the coming of the police the atmosphere changed. To Toby it became something familiar, but to Constance Crane the presence of policemen seemed to add something of dark yet intriguing horror to the death of John Lestarke-Toye. She seemed repelled yet fascinated, and the nervous light in her eyes grew brighter. It was with a look almost of frustration that she obeyed when the inspector asked everyone but Dr. Gayson to leave the room in which the dead man still sat at his desk.

Constance and Toby went into the Tudor dining room.

Sitting down in a high-backed chair at one end of the table, Constance let her hands rest on the carved arms of the chair. Glancing at her hands as they lay there, Toby noticed that the brown stain had gone. As his eyes met hers Constance herself glanced down at her hand, but as soon as she had done it she tried to cancel the unthinking movement by letting her eyelids droop till her eyes were closed.

In the doorway someone cleared his throat. Sir Wilfred Ridden had followed them.

"I wonder if that inspector chap wants me," he said, coming in. "If not, I think I'll be getting home. Daresay I'm only in the way here. Of course, if there's anything I can do to help, I'll stay. What d'you think?" He looked at Toby.

"I'd go if I were you," said Toby.

"Sure? I mean, if I can be of any use . . ."

Almost too obviously impatient, Toby said: "I'd go."

"Right you are," said Ridden. "I'll tootle off. Jove, I

feel all shaken up. I wonder who old John had that fight with, poor old fellow—and I wonder who's got the extra bullet in him now."

Toby said: "I suppose you didn't notice anything unusual about John when you met him?"

"Not a thing—literally not a thing. Oh—wait a minute, though. Did I? Well," said Ridden, "I'm not so sure I didn't. Perhaps he was sort of excited. Yes, I rather think he was. Anyway, he was very short in his replies. Yes, I think definitely he was excited. Yes . . . definitely. But look here, I don't know what I'm thinking of, tootling off and leaving you two here. Where are you going tonight? I suppose you were going to stay here, weren't you? Well, you won't want to do that now, so why not come over to my place? No trouble at all; I can easily arrange something for you. Look, I'll go on ahead and see about it, and then you can follow as soon as they let you go. You take the path through the wood and just keep straight on; you can't miss it."

"It's very kind of you," said Toby, "but I expect there's a pub in the village that——"

"Thank you very much, Sir Wilfred," Constance cut in quickly. "It's very, very kind of you, but I think we shall have to stay here. Suppose Mrs. Lestarke-Toye returned. I don't like to think of the possibility of her coming back and finding things as they are and nobody here to explain or to help her."

"Jove, yes, I hadn't thought of that," said Ridden. "That's fine of you, Miss Crane. You're right, absolutely. Well, then, I'll wander off on my own. If anyone wants me for anything, they know where to find me. Good night—good night, Dyke."

As soon as the door closed on him Toby pulled a chair up to the table and sat down. Through the uncurtained windows he could see the flashlights of the constables. They had just emerged from the house and were moving here and there as if they were searching for something.

"So we're going to stay the night here, are we?" Toby asked ironically.

"I am," Constance replied. "You can do what you like."

"Well, I hope you know what you're doing," he said. "It's obvious you know much more about it all than I do."

"Is it?"

"You know something about J. Porter Ugbrook," he said, "and you know what you were looking for in John's pockets, and you know what happened here earlier this evening—you may even know what's happened to Lili and the servants. So I don't need to waste time telling you that there are one or two things about that scene in there that aren't quite what they seem. I think what we were meant to believe is what Ridden suggested, that John had a fight with someone and shot him—or her— and then died himself as a result of the exertion. But there are a few details that don't fit into that explanation of events, and there's a high probability that the police are going to notice some of them. D'you like the idea of a thorough inquiry, Constance?"

"Why not?" she asked.

"Because I don't," he said. "I don't like seeing my friends in a mess."

"That's very nice of you, Toby," she said, "but you needn't worry. Tell me, what d'you think of that man Ridden? I've just been wondering whether you noticed something that I thought rather strange. Did it strike you that all the time he was here he never asked a single question about Lili?"

"That's true," said Toby, "he didn't."

"Well—isn't it strange?"

"I'm not so sure that it is. You see, I sort of gathered from the doctor that Ridden and Lili supply a good bit of the local scandal. Gayson had just rung him up to ask if she was with him. Ridden was probably feeling self-conscious on the subject."

She shook her head. "I still think it's strange. I've got a sort of feeling that he was afraid to ask where she was."

"You don't think, by any chance, that you're just attributing some of your own fears to him?"

Her eyes blazed at him. "It's true I'm afraid," she said. "I'm very afraid of breaking down and starting to weep and weep and not being able to stop. I feel as if half of my own life had suddenly been blotted out. And yet—isn't it strange, Toby?—I went to America mainly to get away from John. I don't know if you knew that. I managed to find business reasons for going, but what I really went for was to get away from John's complete dependence on me. He always had to have someone to make his decisions for him and push him and prompt him. In time that sort of relationship drains all the life out of you—and of course it was bad for him too. And I suppose I half expected something like Lili to happen to him. But now, somehow . . ."

"What were you hunting for in his pockets, Constance?"

"I'm not going to tell you."

He sighed. "And I suppose you won't tell me anything about J. Porter Ugbrook either?"

"I don't in the least mind telling you all about J. Porter Ugbrook—what I know of him, which isn't much. He's a struggling mystic whose works on Ultimate Reality John suddenly took it into his head to publish. Don't ask me why. You know for some time we've been running a rather paying line in prophecy, phony metaphysics, cheap psychology, and so on. It was John who got it going in the first place, and he'd an uncanny flair for telling what would pay and what wouldn't. I always trusted that flair of his; I used to think the reason it was so good was that he himself was always half taken in by the stuff. But he didn't squander much money on the poor, earnest souls who turned it out. He knew they were generally only too thankful to get into print. If he did sort of yearn after some of their blissful certainties, he always had his head screwed on—until J. Porter Ugbrook came along. Then something went wrong. I took the opportunity John's invitation gave me to come down and try to find out what it was."

"In Ugbrook's room upstairs," said Toby, "I found the remains of an invitation John wrote him. John wrote of needing the help of someone he could trust and of never in the past having had as much help and sympathy as he'd had from Ugbrook."

"But that's almost the same as the letter he sent me," she said.

"Have you got it on you?"

Opening her bag, she searched inside it, then handed him an envelope.

The letter inside was an urgent invitation to Constance to come to Redvers that evening, and it ended in almost the same words as the letter on the hearth in Ugbrook's room.

Handing the letter back, Toby said: "I haven't got mine on me, but it says much the same thing. We're the trusty trio, you, I—and Ugbrook."

"What d'you think it means?"

"Is it possible," said Toby, "that while John, in running that line of books you've been talking about, thought that he'd got his tongue in his cheek, his desire for some comfortably compulsive sort of faith—you're right about that streak in him—suddenly got the better of him, and he began to believe that in J. Porter Ugbrook he'd found the True Prophet?"

"Yes," she replied uneasily, "more than possible. In fact, it might be the explanation of what's happened. You see, Mark Fenning cabled me the terms of the contract John had given Ugbrook. John had kept them to himself for some time, otherwise Mark would have given the alarm sooner. The advance Ugbrook got on his book, *Mind in Unmaking*, was fifteen hundred pounds."

At Toby's exclamation Constance smiled thinly.

Getting to his feet, Toby crossed to the window from where, in the darkness outside, he could still see the torches of the police flickering here and there among the shrubs and trees.

"Don't you know anything else about Ugbrook?" he asked.

She shook her head. Then she corrected herself: "Yes, I do—just one thing. A couple of years ago he lodged for a time at Mrs. Werth's. When Mark Fenning wrote to me about him I recognized the name; I remembered Mrs. Werth talking about a very unsatisfactory lodger whom she'd turned out because he was so dirty. Anyway, why should we bother talking about Ugbrook now, unless—— Toby, was he the person John had the fight with?"

"I believe you could answer that question, but I can't," said Toby. He came back to the table and leaned toward her. "Constance, it's a great pity you won't take me into your confidence. You may want to later, but you'll find it'll get harder and harder to make up your mind to do it. I can tell you those invitations have let us both in for serious trouble."

Her eyes narrowed. "D'you mean they weren't genuine—that it was just someone arranging for us to be here?"

"Oh, I think they're genuine all right," he said, "but, as I've been trying to make you understand all the evening, so is the trouble."

6

THE POLICE questioned Constance first. Later, when Toby's turn came, he was taken to the room where Inspector Rogers had established himself. It was a small room next to the dining room. The inspector, a slow-spoken man whose essentially mild personality was over-shadowed by a mustache of great ferocity, was at a table, writing. Looking up and motioning Toby to a chair, he told him to smoke if he wanted to. A constable sat in the corner of the room with a shorthand pad on his knee.

The inspector asked for Toby's name and address. He went on: "I believe I've heard of you, Mr. Dyke. Aren't you acquainted with Detective Inspector Cust? He's an old friend of mine. I think I've heard him speak of you."

"We've run into each other a number of times," said Toby.

"Ah, I thought so. Well, Mr. Dyke, that being so, I'll tell you what I'll do. I'll begin by telling you a few things. After that I'll ask you to tell me a few."

"Suits me," said Toby.

"First I'll tell you," said Rogers, "that I'll be glad of your co-operation."

"Thanks," said Toby.

"Mind you," said Rogers, "I know you're friends with most of the people mixed up in this business, but so long as I feel sure you're co-operating fairly . . ."

"I understand," said Toby.

"Good. Well, Mr. Dyke, I'll tell you next what Dr. Gayson told me." Rogers glanced down at some notes on the table before him. "He says he feels pretty certain that Mr. Lestarke-Toye died from natural causes. It seems he had a very bad heart, and Dr. Gayson had warned him that any violent exertion might be fatal. Owing to the peculiar circumstances of the death we're going to have a post-mortem, but myself I'm prepared to believe that Dr. Gayson's correct and that Mr. Lestarke-Toye died naturally after somehow overstraining himself. Now it appears that Mr. Lestarke-Toye died in a room in which some sort of violent struggle took place. Presumably he was involved in the struggle himself and died as a result of it. However, we've got to bear in mind that he may have been dead before it happened; he may have come into the room after it had happened; he may have sat and watched it happen. No doubt you've your ideas about that. Now during this struggle somebody—not Mr. Lestarke-Toye, because there are no

wounds on his body—bled heavily onto the carpet. That
somebody, either alive or dead, was then removed from
the scene. He—or she—may have managed to walk away,
though it seems unlikely, because there's no trail of blood
leading in any direction. The point is, there's somebody,
either dead or seriously injured, whom we've got to find.
Until that person's found we aren't going to get very far
with understanding what happened here."

Toby jerked a thumb at the window. "Is that what
your men are hunting for out there?"

"That's right. Not that they'll be able to do much before daylight. Now, Mr. Dyke"—Rogers leaned back in
his chair—"I think I've given you an idea of the line I'm
following. The long and short of it is, I'm keeping an
open mind until I've got a good bit more to go on. Myself, I don't see any point in trying to form a picture of
what happened here while the chief piece in the puzzle
is missing. Find that piece—that's what's got to come first.
But meantime it won't do any harm to fill in a bit of the
background. See what I mean? What I'd like is that you
should give me some general information about the
Lestarke-Toyes—just general information, whether it
strikes you as relevant or not. They've not been in the
neighborhood many months, and I don't know much
about them. And I don't know much about yourself, Mr.
Dyke, nor Miss Crane either."

"I see," said Toby. But, fingering his long chin, he
looked down at the floor. "You remarked yourself on the
fact that I'm friends with most of the people mixed up

in this business. You realize I can't pretend detachment."

"Yes, Mr. Dyke, I do."

"All right then," said Toby. "What d'you want me to tell you?"

"Suppose you begin by telling me how long you've known Mr. Lestarke-Toye."

"I first met John Toye—he didn't bother about the Lestarke in those days," said Toby, "about seven years ago. We were both journalists of sorts; I was crime-reporting, and he was messing around, not too successfully, with musical criticism. He'd messed around with being a novelist already and given it up. Luckily he'd a little money of his own, so it didn't matter much if his stuff didn't go. He was living in rooms in Carberry Square. When I found bugs in my room in Guilford Street I moved in with him. That's how I got to know him as well as I did. The place was run by a Mrs. Werth——"

"Ah yes, Mrs. Werth," said Rogers. "The lady you telephoned this evening when you were inquiring into the whereabouts of Mrs. Lestarke-Toye. Tell me, Mr. Dyke, what made you think she might be with Mrs. Werth?"

"I didn't particularly," said Toby.

"Yet you telephoned."

"Simply because Miss Crane seemed anxious to do something about finding Mrs. Lestarke-Toye. We looked at the names on the telephone pad and just picked one of them."

"But why Mrs. Werth? Didn't it seem to you more likely that Mrs. Lestarke-Toye would be visiting a friend who lived closer at hand?"

"I don't know. Perhaps we picked on Mrs. Werth because her name was the only one we knew."

"Then Mrs. Werth and Mrs. Lestarke-Toye are acquainted?"

"Yes," said Toby, "I believe they know each other very well. I was coming to that. You see, Mrs. Werth isn't quite the ordinary landlady. She's the kind who tells you that she loves having lodgers because she finds people so desperately interesting. She's pretty interesting herself; in fact, she's an uncommonly intelligent woman, though a little fond of uplift, and her cooking's a treat. I'm not sure why I didn't fit in when I stayed there; anyway, I didn't, and I left after a few weeks. But the place suited John Toye to perfection. He was the kind of man who loves it when elderly women with sensibility take an interest in his welfare, and as his mother had died only a short time before, Mrs. Werth just stepped in and took her place. Her husband was Karl Werth, the cellist; you may have heard of him. He died about ten years ago, but he was pretty famous in his time. So Mrs. Werth was able to get Toye the introductions that gave him a chance with his musical criticism, and I think she more or less told him what to write. He was always going to concerts with her and used to spend most of his evenings with the family. I daresay he'd be at Carberry Square still if he hadn't run into Miss Crane."

"Of the firm of Banner and Crane—she's been telling

me about that. Seems she met him and gave him a job and about a year later took him into partnership. What you might call a quick change in his fortunes. Would you have said"—Rogers looked up from his notes—"that it was all due to ability?"

"Most of it," said Toby dryly.

Rogers smiled. "You don't need to be too guarded, Mr. Dyke. Miss Crane herself is a very frank lady. She told me of her relations with Mr. Lestarke-Toye."

"Then why ask me what his rise was due to? All the same," said Toby, "ability did come into it. As she's put it herself, he had flair. He always had that queer kind of perceptiveness that makes some people very slick at recognizing what has the seeds of success in it. Even so, it was always Miss Crane who had to take decisions, and it was she who uprooted him from Mrs. Werth's and pushed him into a flat of his own. I rather doubt if Mrs. Werth ever quite forgave her."

"And I suppose," said Rogers, "that it's from Banner and Crane he gets his money? He must be pretty well-to-do to live in a house like this." He glanced around at stippled walls and metallic garnishings. "Fine place," he commented.

"An almost unspoiled specimen of Early Gaumont. However," said Toby, "it wasn't on Banner and Crane that he managed it. Some months ago a relative of Toye's died and left him a lot of money. It was then he bought this house."

"I take it by then he was married?"

"He married last April," said Toby.

"Thank you, Mr. Dyke," said Rogers. "And now please tell me what you know about Mrs. Lestarke-Toye."

Toby shook his head. "I'm afraid I know scarcely anything about her."

"But you've met her, haven't you?"

"Once."

"Perhaps you would describe her."

Toby considered. "Well, she's uncommonly beautiful —one of those blondes that——"

"Blondes?" Rogers interrupted. "Miss Crane said she was dark and Spanish-looking."

"She was blonde when I saw her," said Toby.

"Excuse me, sir," said the constable in the corner. "The last time as I saw Mrs. Lestarke-Toye 'er 'air was horburn."

"I see," said Rogers. "Well, please go on, Mr. Dyke."

Toby said irritably: "But I tell you, I know next to nothing about her."

"Not even—for instance—how she and Mr. Lestarke-Toye became acquainted?"

"Oh, yes," said Toby, "I know that. It was Mrs. Werth who introduced them. Mrs. Lestarke-Toye had lodged at Carberry Square once with her first husband, and she went back there after he died. I believe he was killed in a railway accident. Mrs. Lestarke-Toye—that's to say, Mrs. Snape, though she was calling herself Miss Dános—settled in at Mrs. Werth's and tried to get into the films. She'd got as far as a few small parts when she gave it up and married."

"And you saw her at the wedding?"

"No, I wasn't at the wedding."

"Then when did you see her?"

"I saw her at a party which the Lestarke-Toyes gave as a sort of farewell to the flat they were living in just before they moved down here. The whole affair was rather embarrassing, because Mrs. Lestarke-Toye was obviously annoyed at my being there. I got the impression that she didn't want her husband to go on seeing any of his former friends, particularly any who were also friends of Miss Crane's. I suppose, in a way, it was quite understandable. Toye himself was in a dithery sort of state; I couldn't understand it. He tried to talk to me several times, but by the time he'd said how long it was since we'd seen each other, his wife always managed to chip in. I've been wondering whether I was asked to that party for the same reason as I believe I was asked down here—that's to say, whether there wasn't something on Toye's mind which he wanted to discuss with a friend he could trust."

"You think that Mrs. Lestarke-Toye was anxious to prevent it?"

"I don't know about that."

"Was a man called J. Porter Ugbrook at that party?" asked Rogers.

"No."

Tapping his pencil against the fine white teeth that showed under his bulky mustache, Rogers remained silent. But after a moment, still tapping his teeth, he went on: "I suppose, Mr. Dyke, that you took a bit of a look round here before us or the doctor turned up? I shouldn't wonder if you noticed a thing or two, eh?"

"I shouldn't wonder," said Toby.

"That paper spill in the grate in Ugbrook's room, for instance. I shouldn't wonder if you noticed that."

"You're perfectly right, I did," said Toby.

"And then there was the bath water in Mr. Lestarke-Toye's bathroom."

Toby nodded. "I noticed also," he said, "that the wireless was on when I arrived, soon after nine o'clock, and that the light in that room where it all happened wasn't."

"Ah," said Rogers, "where it all happened. Quite so. But where what happened—and did it all happen there, eh? You know, Mr. Dyke, it's a very odd situation, it's really very odd indeed. We've a scene of violence and a dead man in the middle of it, yet the dead man's died a natural death."

"I agree, it's very odd," said Toby. He stood up. As no more questions came he turned to the door. "What you've got on your hands is a corpse without a murder and a murder without a corpse."

"Which, if you ask me, is absurd," said Inspector Rogers.

7

It was late in the night when the house grew quiet. When at last the police departed they left seals on the door of the wrecked room. An ambulance came for the body of John Lestarke-Toye. Dr. Gayson went home.

Saying that she was hungry, Constance went to the kitchen to look for something to eat, and presently she reappeared with coffee and a plate of sandwiches. She took them into the dining room. Sitting there, however, sipping the coffee and nibbling at a sandwich, she showed no signs of the hunger of which she had spoken. She looked very tired.

Once or twice Toby tried to talk to her, but she scarcely paid attention. When she had smoked one cigarette she rose abruptly, said good night, and went up to one of the rooms that had been prepared. Toby finished off the sandwiches and coffee, then he, too, went upstairs.

The room he chose faced Constance's across the purple-carpeted landing. Switching on the electric fire, he glanced over the books on the shelves by the bed. They were mostly Banner and Crane productions, still in new, brightly colored jackets. Picking out a novel called *Cheers for the Hangman*, he was returning with it to the fire when his eye fell on a slim book which lay on its side on an otherwise empty shelf. The book was *Mind in Unmaking*, by J. Porter Ugbrook.

Replacing the thriller, Toby took back with him to the chair by the fire the book for which John Lestarke-Toye had paid fifteen hundred pounds. He flicked over the pages. The frontispiece of the book was a photograph of the author. It showed a man of about forty-five, with a square, heavy face, a high, bald forehead, and tufts of bushy gray hair curling over the ears. The features were blunt and powerful. The eyes under the shaggy, frowning brows had a look of deliberately sustained concentration. Certainly there was something dynamic about the face, but whether it was dynamic intelligence or merely dynamic vanity the photograph was not able to reveal. Toby turned the pages. While the cold bedroom slowly filled with warmth he sat there, reading the work of the vanished writer.

There were not more than twenty thousand words in the volume. They appeared to deal with the advantages of being more or less without consciousness and with techniques for achieving this condition. The new moon, sexual continence, and a vegetarian diet were all of great importance. Toby soon found the words cascading past his understanding and leaving no impression on him but a deep mental lassitude. This was increased by his tiredness. With his head dropping back against the chair and with his eyelids feeling heavier with every moment, he found sentence after sentence slithering past his comprehension. But he did not fall asleep. When a door on the landing was cautiously opened he was wide awake in an instant.

Swiftly crossing the room, he put his ear to the crack of the door. He heard soft footfalls on the carpet outside, then the sound of the opening of another door. When a minute had gone by he quietly edged his own door open.

From the doorway next to his own a narrow line of light fell across the landing. It was the doorway of the room that had been made ready for J. Porter Ugbrook. The door was ajar, and now and then the line of light was blotted out by the shadow of someone moving about inside the room.

Toby stepped out onto the landing and went to the door. For a little while he stood there watching, then he walked into the room. He asked wearily: "Constance, what the ruddy hell d'you think you're playing at?"

As before, when he had caught her searching the pockets of John Lestarke-Toye, Constance Crane sprang backward with a frightened gasp. The contents of the suitcase she had been searching were mostly on the floor. Toby looked down at them.

"I've already been through this suitcase myself," he said. "There's nothing of any interest in it."

Constance, wearing a blue velvet wrapper, with her fair hair loose on her shoulders, stared at him with eyes that blazed out of circles of dark shadow. There was a rasp of anxiety in her voice: "You say you've already looked through?"

"Yes. However, I took nothing out of it."

Quickly she went to work on the suitcase again. Toby sat down on the edge of the bed and waited while she shook out shirts and socks and handkerchiefs. Her lips were bitten into a hard line. She took no notice of him. When the suitcase was empty she stood still with a nervous frown on her face. Then she went to work on the chest of drawers and cupboards.

Toby, crossing his legs, sat and watched her. Presently he remarked: "I suppose this was why you wanted to stay the night?"

She banged a cupboard door. "Did you think it was for the pleasure of your company?"

"That'd have been a wholesomer reason."

"I'm sorry to disappoint you. It'd suit me excellently at the moment to be alone."

"I hope you've taken into consideration the fact that the police have certainly been through this place with a fine comb."

"I don't think they've removed what I'm looking for." She hurried on to the next cupboard.

Smiling, but with eyes that were somber, he said: "You haven't got some fool notion of finding that fifteen-hundred-pound contract and destroying it, have you, Constance?"

She answered impatiently: "Of course not. It was witnessed as well as signed. Besides, people don't travel around with their contracts in their pockets."

"Then what is it you want to get your hands on?"

"Nothing."

He sighed. "And I used to think you one of the saner women of my acquaintance."

"What's wrong with my sanity?"

"Nothing!" he said.

"Well," she said, turning away dispiritedly from the last cupboard, "I *don't* want to get my hands on anything—except, if you keep on interfering like this, your throat, dear Toby."

"Hunting pretty hard for nothing, aren't you?"

"No—I'm looking for something, but I don't want to remove it when I find it. I merely want to see if it's there."

"Sorry," said Toby. "I ought to have understood your very lucid explanation straight away."

She gave him a furious glance, then once more she looked round the room. "No," she muttered, "I don't think I've missed out anywhere."

"If you call that a thorough search," said Toby, "you've still a lot to learn. You haven't looked under the carpet or under the mattress or up the chimney."

"Oh, for heaven's sake, Toby!" Her fingers curled like claws. "I wonder if you'd mind not actually *trying* to get on my nerves. They're edgy enough already."

"If you'd tell me what you're looking for, I might be able to find it for you," he suggested.

"No, it isn't here. You see, it wouldn't be hidden, it'd simply be among Ugbrook's things. I was looking through those drawers and cupboards just to make sure he hadn't taken any of his things out of his suitcase and put them away already."

"So whatever it is, he's taken it with him, has he?"

She did not answer

Toby stood up. "All right then, if the fun's over I'll be getting back to bed. But, Constance——" He came to her and put his hands on her shoulders. "Constance, what's the trouble? Why don't you tell me?"

He could feel her hesitation in the tension of her muscles. At length, in a low voice, she replied: "Because I've done something insane—something desperately, dangerously insane, Toby. I don't want you to be involved in it."

"I was afraid that might be it."

She dropped her eyes. "I—I was so fond of John, it seemed the natural thing to do, but of course, as soon as I'd had time to think . . ." She made a gesture with her hands as if she had explained everything. "I can't undo it," she went on, twisting her fingers together. "Even if I realize now how mad I was, all I can do is wait and see what happens—and see that no one else gets mixed up in my madness. So don't—please don't go on asking me questions, Toby. My mind's made up about answering them."

"All right," said Toby, "no more questions."

As if surprised at his acquiescence, she looked into his face, then said, sighing: "I can see you don't mean it. Oh well . . ." She turned to the door. "About what I was looking for—it really isn't anything very important, and as you said, I expect Ugbrook's got it with him. I was looking for it only because . . . Well, it's rather queer that it isn't there, that's all."

"All right—that's all." He grinned. "Good night, Constance."

"Good night, Toby."

"By the way," he said as she put a hand on the door, "I've been reading *Mind in Unmaking*, and I completely endorse everything you've said about the queerness of John's having lost his head over the man who wrote it. But if you're afraid that when you get to bed you won't be able to sleep, let me recommend that book as ten times better than aspirins. And—just one thing more, Constance. I'm not going to ask you any more questions until I know the answers. It'll be harder work that way, but I realize it's the only thing to do. I know a stubborn woman when I see one."

8

It was another stubborn woman, thumping strong-mindedly on his door, who awakened Toby the next morning. She kept on with her thumping until at last his voice, husky with sleep, growled something out from under the bedclothes, then she opened the door briskly, said: "You're wanted on the telephone, sir," and disappeared again. Toby, staggering out of bed into dressing gown and slippers, was left to puzzle out with his sleep-fogged brain how it could be that a house which by night had been deserted and neglected should in the morning blossom out with so perfect a specimen of the domestic servant—frilled cap, starched apron, all complete.

On the way downstairs he smelled coffee and bacon. Through the open door of the dining room he saw that the table had been laid and that a big fire was burning on the hearth. He stood at the foot of the stairs, rubbing his eyes and trying to remember where he had seen a telephone other than the one in the sealed room. Just then the woman who had wakened him passed through the hall. She was a round, elderly woman with crinkled, rosy cheeks. Seeing him hesitating, she directed him into the little room where he had sat and talked with Inspector Rogers.

It was Mrs. Werth on the telephone. Toby recognized her deep, rather rough voice the moment she started to speak.

"I'm sorry I wasn't in last night when you telephoned, Toby," she said. "Billy told me about it. He said you said it was something important."

"That's right," said Toby, "it is. In fact, it's a lot worse than important. D'you mind telling me, Mrs. Werth, have you any idea where Lili's got to?"

"Of course," said Mrs. Werth. "She's here."

"She is? But Billy said——"

"To be precise, she's looking at me from across the room. She's in the middle of breakfast. D'you want to speak to her?"

"No," said Toby quickly, "no, I don't. I want to speak to you, Mrs. Werth."

"You see, Billy didn't know anything about it," Mrs. Werth went on. "He was in bed all day. He ate about seven mince pies, so bed was the only place for him. But what's the matter, Toby? From your voice, it's something serious."

"I said it was, didn't I? Look, Mrs. Werth"—Toby cleared his throat—"this is a devilish thing to have to throw at a person over the telephone, but I've got to do it. And then, I'm afraid, you'll have to break it to Lili. John—well, he's dead."

He heard her quick gasp. Then followed a silence.

After a moment he said anxiously: "Mrs. Werth . . ."

Her voice came jerkily: "It's all right. I heard what you said." There was another slight pause, then she added: "Please go on."

"That's all, really."

"But how? When?"

"The doctor thinks it happened round about six o'clock yesterday evening. It was his heart, of course. Seems it just went."

"Toby, there's something you're keeping from me."

"What makes you think so, Mrs. Werth?"

"You're being so unnaturally terse."

"Oh, I don't know . . . I'm always terse before breakfast."

"Toby, please!"

"Really, Mrs. Werth, there isn't much else I can tell you over the telephone. One's got to say either too much or too little. Will you please tell Lili what I've told you and then, if she's up to it, bring her down here?"

"Yes, yes, of course. But, Toby, there *is* something you're keeping from me, isn't there?"

"Well, did I mention that Constance is here? But I expect Lili knows that. By the way, did you happen to notice yesterday what time it was when Lili arrived at your house?"

"I didn't notice it specially. I think it was around six. Why?" Her voice sharpened: "Is *that* important? Then there *is* something . . . ?"

"You couldn't say more definitely how near to six it was?"

"Well, it wasn't many minutes after six, because I'd just gone down to the kitchen to put the stew on when she came, and I know it was six o'clock when I went down. She went to a concert with me after supper. I'd meant to take Billy, but he was in bed, so I'd a spare ticket. Oh, Toby, how terrible it is! I feel as if . . . But that's no good; I'll try not to say what I feel. I'll—I'll do what you asked me."

"And you'll bring Lili down here?"

"As soon as I can. Good-by, Toby."

"Good-by, Mrs. Werth."

About a quarter of an hour later, when Toby, dressed, came downstairs again, he found that Constance had appeared. She looked as if she had not slept; on the pallor and slackness of her skin the make-up showed with unpleasant harshness. With obvious difficulty she was eating a small triangle of toast and marmalade and drinking black coffee.

Toby said as he sat down: "Well, Lili's found."

"Where?" But Constance did not sound very interested.

"At Mrs. Werth's," said Toby. "She was there all the

time. Thanks"—as Constance handed him a cup of coffee. "It's rather pleasant, isn't it, that we acquired a domestic staff during the night? Where d'you think it came from?"

"I take such things as favors from heaven," said Constance.

"Well, then, suppose you push that bell," said Toby, "I think you can just reach it—and let me inquire how heaven worked it."

She looked at him bleakly. "Do you really mean to say you can't even sit and have breakfast in peace before you start asking questions? Isn't it enough for you that fires have been lit and that good food and drink's ready for you—and that the police have a habit of doing their own work quite competently? Can't you digest all that in thankfulness and keep quiet for a little?"

"Sorry, Constance." He helped himself to bacon and eggs. "Suppose the good fairy vanished away while I was busy digesting?"

"She won't."

"You can never be certain."

Sighing, she reached for the bell.

"And have you decided," she asked as she struggled on with her seemingly inedible triangle of toast, "whose blood it is on the carpet if it isn't Lili's?"

"J. Porter Ugbrook is the other person who's missing, isn't he?"

She shuddered slightly. But before she could speak again the domestic staff, entering with a rustle of starched print, appeared in the doorway.

Toby began: "Good morning."

The woman replied briskly: "Good morning, sir."

"We're rather curious," said Toby, "to know who you are and how you got here—or, if you prefer, why you weren't here yesterday evening. I wonder if you could tell us how that came about."

"Certainly, sir." There was an earnestness in the woman's briskness which showed that she was giving due thought to the fact that there had been death in the house. "The reason there was no one here yesterday— no servants, that is—was that Mrs. Lestarke-Toye had given us all notice."

"What—yesterday?"

"Yes sir, yesterday afternoon—though really what I mean is, she didn't give us notice. She gave us a month's wages and told us all to go."

Toby exchanged glances with Constance. "Didn't she give any reason?"

"No sir."

"Just told you to leave straight away?"

"Yes sir."

"And you've absolutely no idea why?"

"As to that—well, I never said that," said the woman.

"Ah." Toby swiveled his chair a little so as to face her more directly. "By the way, would you mind telling us your name, Mrs.——"

"Tomlinson, sir. I'm cook here, and I'm a Mallowby woman. That's how I come to be here this morning and not the others, because Gladys and Parkes both went away to their homes. Parkes—he was butler and chauffeur—he went off to London, and Gladys went home to St. Albans. But I live in Mallowby, so that's how I come to be here, you see."

"Yes, but why, Mrs. Tomlinson?" asked Toby. "I mean, if you were given notice, what made you come back?"

"It was the police, sir. That isn't to say they made me come, but late last night the inspector came in to see me and ask me just these questions you've been asking me yourself, about why we wasn't here, any of us, and all that. And he told me all about the shocking death of poor Mr. Lestarke-Toye and about you and Miss Crane being here with no one to look after you. And so I thought, well, even if I have been given my notice, I thought, I'll just pop up and put things a bit to rights, because I'm sure poor Mr. Lestarke-Toye wouldn't like his friends to be neglected."

"That was very kind of you, Mrs. Tomlinson," said Toby. "But about your ideas of why Mrs. Lestarke-Toye gave you notice—I suppose you told the police about that?"

Uneasiness appeared on Mrs. Tomlinson's face. "Yes, I did tell the inspector—but that's different like from telling you and madam. I mean, well, I don't hardly *like* to tell you"—she glanced from one to the other—"all along of its being something to do with you. You see, it was on account of Mr. Lestarke-Toye asking friends to stay without telling her anything about it that Mrs. Lestarke-Toye flew into a temper and they had that quarrel. A terrible quarrel it was—and how Mrs. Lestarke-

Toye must be regretting it now, poor soul, though maybe she made her peace with him before she went away. She was always one for quarreling, and him always as mild as could be, though I will say this for her, it was always just her temper; one minute she'd be screaming at him, and the next minute it'd all be over. Maybe that's what happened yesterday. But I do know they quarreled something terrible when she found that Gladys had put the spare bedrooms ready on Mr. Lestarke-Toye's orders, and when she found out—begging your pardon—who it was expected, she went right down frantic. We could hear the things they was saying to each other out in the kitchen."

"They didn't actually fight over it, I suppose?" said Toby. "It wasn't they who knocked that room about?"

"Oh no, sir!" said Mrs. Tomlinson, shocked. "It was all quite refined, except for a few of the words she used, but she was always a very modern lady, so we've got used to that. After a bit he just said he couldn't stand any more of it and he walked straight out into the garden and then set off toward the woods as if he was going for a walk. She stayed by herself for a bit, and then suddenly she walks into the kitchen and gives us all notice. Tells us to stop everything we're doing and pack up and go. She's laughing to herself and says he can have his friends, she says, he can have the whole blooming lot—begging your pardon—and they can look after themselves and see how they like that, she says. Then she gives us all our money and says we can all write to her for references, and she stands watching while we pack, and she has us all out of the house in no more than half an hour. I said to Gladys as we was waiting out there for the bus, I said I don't hardly know if I'm on my head or my feet. To tell the truth, I still feel kind of upset by the whole experience. I was in my last place twelve years."

"And what time did all this happen, Mrs. Tomlinson?" asked Toby.

"Well, it was the five-o'clock bus Gladys and Parkes caught. Of course I was only going to Mallowby, so I saw them off and then I walked home. I left my boxes under the hedge, and my brother came later with his cart and collected them. I think it must've been about half-past four when Mrs. Lestarke-Toye walked into the kitchen and told us to go."

"And didn't you see Mrs. Lestarke-Toye herself leave for London?"

"No sir. But then Mallowby's the other way, so I wouldn't see her."

"I see. Thanks very much," said Toby. "It's made things a lot clearer."

As Mrs. Tomlinson went out Constance, sitting with her elbows on the table, nursing her cup in her hands, looked at Toby with raised eyebrows and asked ironically: "Has it?"

"It has," said Toby.

"Don't try to impress me," she said. "I'm too used to you; it just slides off."

Getting up, crossing to the fireplace, and using the poker to stir the fire into a livelier blaze, he said: "It makes at least one point clear. Mrs. Werth says that Lili

arrived at Carberry Square at about six o'clock; that
means that Lili must have left here soon after five. She
left after the servants—probably not many minutes after.
As John had left the house before the servants and met
Ridden at the bottom of the hill at about half-past five,
the house must have been empty for at least three quarters of an hour. Unless"—he hesitated—"unless that's the
time when Ugbrook and the other person arrived."

"What other person?" she asked quickly.

"That's what I don't know. But between the time
Lili and the servants left and the time I turned up, at least
three people had been in this house. John, Ugbrook, and
—somebody."

"But how d'you know that?"

He looked round at her, smiling blandly. "It's you
who want to know a lot this morning, isn't it, Constance?
Of course, if you'd consider a pooling of information . . ."

Pushing her chair back sharply, she stood up.

"I suppose," she said, "you're still dropping hints
about that stain you thought you saw on my nail."

"Did I only think I saw it?"

"Yes."

"All right," he answered, laughing. "The police
needn't know I suffer from delusions. However, it wasn't
that stain I was thinking about at all. There are other
indications that at least three people were here during
that time. *At least* three. But there may have been any
number more."

"Are you thinking of that man Ridden?"

"At present it'd be premature to think of anyone in particular."

She made an impatient movement. Stooping, Toby poked the fire again. When he straightened up he found she was looking at him with a gaze of probing intensity. But she said nothing more, and after a short silence she crossed to the door.

Toby said: "By the way, Lili and Mrs. Werth will be arriving shortly."

She merely nodded and went out. Toby glanced at his watch. Seeing that there was no possibility of Lili and Mrs. Werth arriving for at least half an hour, he returned to the table, poured out another cup of coffee, gulped it, went into the hall, put on his overcoat, and walked out into the frozen garden.

For the first time he looked at the house by daylight. At the hysterical jumble of flints, bricks, and Portland stone, of gables and bays and Ionic columns that gibbered at him in pure architectural lunacy, he made a rude noise. Then he walked off across the lawn. The grass, brittle with frost, crunched under his shoes. He walked toward the wood. He found, when he reached it, that it was only a small plantation covering a gently sloping hillside, with a path running downward through the trees. Stopping first to light a cigarette, he started down the path, but only a few yards along it, where a gap framed by two hollies gave him a view of the meadows that spread out at the foot of the hill, he stood still again.

For some minutes he remained staring through the gap

at the house that faced him across the meadows. His eyes had narrowed. He might have been admiring the mellow brick and the quiet firmness of line about the old walls and the low-pitched roof, the sane proportions, and the stolid, eighteenth-century dignity; or he might have been calculating how many minutes it would take to cross from Redvers to the home of Sir Wilfred Ridden. . . .

The path, when it left the wood, led him to a stile in a hedge, beyond which he found a rough cart track. In any other weather the track would have been slimy with mud, but today the frost had hardened the surface and made the ruts as firm as trolley rails.

Toby climbed the stile. In the opposite hedge was another stile, beyond which the path continued toward the Ridden mansion. Thoughtfully considering the house again, Toby hesitated between the two stiles, but after a moment he continued down the track, which changed, when it reached the main gates of the Ridden estate, into a metaled road that brought him in a few minutes to the fork where he had stopped his car on the previous evening. On his left, against a background of the bare boughs of apple trees, was the white cottage he had seen through the darkness.

Someone was chopping wood behind the cottage. Edging round outside the fence that enclosed the orchard, Toby came on a tall old man standing in the doorway of a shed, splitting logs with a hatchet. When the old man saw Toby he straightened his back.

" 'Tis a cold mornin'," he observed.

Toby agreed that it was perishing cold. They discussed the cold weather minutely.

Presently Toby inquired if the old man had heard of the death up at Redvers.

Hogben said: "Ay," adding that he had had it from the milkman, whose sister was married to Mrs. Tomlinson's brother.

"An unfortunate business," said Toby, leaning on the fence.

"Ay," said the old man again, adding with gloomy detachment: "And it'll be my turn next, I reckon. A good job, too, with the world the way it is. I shan't be the one to grumble when they take me out feet foremost."

"Sir Wilfred Ridden says he met Mr. Lestarke-Toye just outside your gate yesterday evening," said Toby.

"Ay, that he did," said Hogben. "Sir Wilfred he'd been in to see me about my roof—but you can take it from me, he won't do nothin'."

"Then you saw Mr. Lestarke-Toye yourself, did you?" asked Toby.

"Ay," said Hogben, "I did."

"Going which way?"

"Comin' along the lower road and goin' for to climb the hill."

"How was it you saw him?" asked Toby. "It was dark, wasn't it?"

Hogben gave a creaky laugh. "Was it Inspector Rogers who learned you all these questions, mister? They're the very same ones he was askin' me an hour since. Ay, 'twas dark, but I was lightin' Sir Wilfred to the gate with my lantern, and I sees Toye goin' by and I calls out and says: ' 'Tis a cold evenin'.' "

"And about what time would that be?"

Hogben chuckled again. "I reckon you're one o' they plain-clothes policemen, eh?—even if you don't wear no bowler hat. 'Twas half-past five, as near as may be."

"You're sure of that?"

"Ay, mister, I can tell the time."

Toby grinned. "Yes—but what made you happen to notice it?"

The old man considered. "I reckon 'twas the bus goin' by—the bus from London. I sees 'er go by from the window just after I come in and shut the door. She goes by at thirty-five minutes past the hour."

"I see," said Toby. "Thanks."

"You're welcome," said Hogben. " 'Tis a cold mornin'."

"Perishing cold," said Toby.

Hesitating by which of the two roads to return to the house, he set off up the hill.

He found it was the longer as well as the steeper route. The gray in the sky was clearing and a wintry blue was showing through the clouds. When he reached the house he looked through the downstairs rooms for Constance, but Mrs. Tomlinson told him that Miss Crane was in her bedroom. Returning to the dining room, Toby pulled a chair close to the fire and for some time sat there smoking and staring into the flames and now and then looking at his watch.

Presently he started searching through his pockets and,

from the miscellaneous handful he brought out, selected an old envelope and a pencil. But as soon as the pencil touched the paper he checked the movement to write. His gaze went back to the fire, and when he used the pencil it was only to scrawl a pattern of daisies round the edges of the envelope. When at length the sound of a car on the drive roused him from his thoughts he glanced at the envelope, muttered: "Hell, this isn't going to get me anywhere!" and threw it into the fire. A moment later he was opening the front door as Lili Lestarke-Toye came slowly up the steps.

9

THE BEAUTY of Lili Lestarke-Toye had some of the quality of high explosive: it made a big bang on impact; if, however, the beholder was not instantaneously knocked out by it, he was liable to find it relatively easy to regain his normal balance. Lili herself was grandly convinced of her own beauty. The conviction gave her poise but also a sort of brooding blankness of expression. Her face was longish, wide at the cheekbones and sloping in sharply to a small, pointed chin. She was tall and always moved with careful grace and a schooled display of the fine curves of her body. Today she was wearing a belted camel-hair coat and was hatless; her auburn hair fell sleekly onto her shoulders. If she had wept at her husband's death it had soon been over, for her features were unmarred.

When she saw Toby she slightly inclined her head then walked past him into the house.

Paying only a very little more attention to her than she had to him, Toby turned to Mrs. Werth, who came pattering up the steps behind Lili.

A small, shriveled woman, Mrs. Werth looked shrunken and rather sickly inside a shabby musquash coat. She had a hat made of velvet and what looked like crystallized violets perched on her dyed black hair. She had bold, intelligent black eyes and a slight hump between her shoulders. As always, there was something vividly, nervously alive about her.

Thrusting a claw of a hand into Toby's, she whispered: "Poor girl, she's stunned. She's scarcely said a word. I had to drive the car, and yet I think I've been crying more than she has. Oh, Toby, isn't it terrible— *terrible?*"

"It's a good thing she had you with her," said Toby.

"Yes, I'm so thankful she came to me yesterday. The silly things, they had a quarrel, and now, of course, she feels that that was a sort of crime. It's tragic, isn't it? Oh, why do these things have to happen?" Giving his hand a squeeze, Mrs. Werth pattered on after Lili.

Toby was turning to follow her when he realized that someone else had got out of the car. A girl, smallish and sallow, with wiry brown hair and sullen eyes, was mounting the steps.

Toby said: "Hullo, Leora."

The girl did not look up as she greeted him. Letting

her hand lie limply in his for a moment, she went on after her mother.

Following them inside, Toby said: "There's a fire in the dining room."

But no one moved in that direction, for an instant after he had spoken Constance Crane appeared on the staircase.

In Constance's face, as she looked down and saw Lili Lestarke-Toye in the hall below, there appeared at first a softening of pity. It was as if Constance felt for a moment that they had a grief to share and to lighten for one another. But before she had reached the bottom of the stairs her face had gone as cold and as unrevealing as Lili's. The two of them met with complete artificiality.

Lili held out a hand and said: "I'm so glad to see you again, Constance. It was most kind of you to stay. John told me such a lot about you; I always wanted to know you better." Her voice had a flat, fluty quality, as if some accent had been carefully drilled out of it. Their hands touched, then Lili's hand was abruptly withdrawn. She followed Mrs. Werth and Leora into the dining room.

Mrs. Werth spoke excitedly: "Toby, you must tell us exactly what's happened. You must tell us everything. It's terrible, this half knowing."

First Toby looked questioningly at Lili. She had just sat down, had crossed her legs gracefully, and was unbuttoning her coat.

"Please," she said briefly, nodding, "I should like to know everything."

"Just one moment," Mrs. Werth went on quickly, her little yellow face working. "Where is he, Toby? I mean—where's John?"

"I was just going to explain about that," said Toby. "I'm afraid he's not here any more. You see, there's going to be an inquest."

Lili's eyes widened a little.

Mrs. Werth gasped: "An inquest? But that means——"

"It means that the police—and Dr. Gayson—aren't satisfied," said Toby.

"Oh, Lili, my dear!" moaned Mrs. Werth, her hand tightening convulsively on the younger woman's arm.

A shade of irritation crossed Lili's face. "Please tell us the rest of it as quickly as you can," she said to Toby.

He told them of his arrival. He told them of how he had found John, of the condition of the room, of how he had telephoned for Dr. Gayson. Sitting motionless, ignoring Mrs. Werth's exclamations and little, fluttering gestures, Lili kept her eyes on his face. It was not until he had told them of how Dr. Gayson had spoken of John's expectation of death that, suddenly altering her pose and speaking in a voice of husky intensity, she said: "Yes, yes, John and I, we both knew. Oh, my God, we knew—I knew—and yet I let that foolish quarrel come between us. The last words John and I ever spoke were spoken in anger." She moved her gaze slowly from one face to the other. "Shall I ever be able to forget that?"

Mrs. Werth said at once: "You mustn't let that prey on your mind, Lili. What do your words matter? It's your love for each other you must remember."

"But don't you understand," said Lili, motionless again in the new pose, "it was that quarrel that killed him? I killed him."

"Lili, I've told you already not to say such things," said Mrs. Werth sharply. "Don't say them, don't think them. They aren't true, and they might be dangerous—if I've understood Toby correctly, that's to say. Am I right, Toby?"

"Undoubtedly," he answered.

"Dangerous!" said Lili with a kind of laugh. "What does that matter? I tell you, if we hadn't quarreled—if I hadn't made that quarrel—nothing would have happened. I'm sure nothing would have happened. I'm going to have that thought with me for the rest of my life."

Mrs. Werth frowned. "But you haven't told us the whole of it yet, have you, Toby?"

"Haven't I?" he said. "I can only tell you what I saw myself, but I daresay you can get a lot more from the police."

"I feel there's something you're keeping back," said Mrs. Werth.

"Well . . . I don't believe I mentioned the strange disappearance of J. Porter Ugbrook, did I?"

"What—that horrible man!" cried Mrs. Werth. "You don't mean he was here?"

"He was here at some time yesterday evening," said Toby.

"Then when did he disappear?"

Toby shrugged his shoulders.

"But . . ." She sat down abruptly. She looked

blanched and shaken. "You aren't being frank with us, Toby. You're dropping hints and looking mysterious instead of speaking straightforwardly. It isn't kind. You ought to think of what Lili's suffering. We're none of us in a fit state to solve puzzles. It's been a dreadful shock to us all. What made you mention that man? What's he done? Why did your voice go so unconvincingly casual when you spoke of him? Are you—are you trying to tell us that it was he whom John fought with?—because that's what you meant when you were describing the state of the room, wasn't it? You meant that two people had a fight there, and—well, was it John and Ugbrook?"

"I don't know," said Toby.

"But it is what you think, isn't it?" she pressed him.

"I've just said I don't know."

"Toby, for God's sake——"

"Oh, what does it matter?" said Lili irritably. "I hope John fought with him, and I hope he killed him. He'd have liked to kill him, I know."

There was a startled silence.

As the silence lasted Lili went on calmly: "Of course Ugbrook was blackmailing John."

For another moment no one spoke, then Constance said harshly: "To be blackmailed you've got to have done something—blackmailable!"

Lili looked at her with a smile. "And don't you think John ever had? And I thought you knew him so well! However, I can show you a letter—a letter from Ugbrook. Not that it'll tell you what his hold was; he was too clever to put that in writing. But John kept it carefully, in case someday he could turn it against Ugbrook. It's here in the safe." Rising and moving with her usual deliberate grace, she took a couple of steps to the side of the fireplace. As she pressed on the wall a panel swung forward. It revealed a small safe let into the wall behind. Toby, who had come quickly to her side, saw her twist the knobs, and as the door of the safe came open he saw as soon as she did that the safe was empty.

Lili said nothing. She merely went on looking into the cavity, then, with a shrug, she turned to face the others.

Toby asked: "Was there anything else in the safe besides the letter?"

"I don't know," said Lili, going back to her chair.

"It's not much of a safe," said Toby. "The best thing about it is the way it's concealed in the wall. How many people knew of its existence?"

"I don't know," she said again.

"Well, your letter's gone all right—like Ugbrook."

"I don't believe any of it!" said Leora suddenly.

Her mother jerked round to look at her. Lili raised her eyebrows a trifle. Toby said thoughtfully: "Don't you, Leora?"

Keeping her eyes on the ground, Leora said hurriedly: "I don't believe there's a letter. I don't believe there ever was one. Constance is quite right: to be blackmailed you've first got to do something discreditable, and—oh, you knew John as well as I did. John was much too cautious and virtuous ever to do anything to be ashamed of."

Lili said ironically: "Leora, my dear, you're a child."

"Very well then," snapped Leora, "what was it he'd done?"

"That's a question you've no right to ask," said her mother. "None of us has a right to ask it."

"Oh, I shouldn't mind telling you—if I knew," said Lili. "But, you see, I don't. I daresay you think that's rather funny. Perhaps it is. Most wives pry into their husband's business, don't they? But it just happens I didn't."

With a puzzled look Constance said: "You mean you knew that John was being blackmailed, yet you didn't know what for?"

"Yes," said Lili, "that is what I mean. I never pressed John to tell me more about his past life than he was ready to tell me without persuasion."

Flushing, Constance insisted: "You mean John told you he was being blackmailed, yet he didn't——"

"No, I never said John told me he was being blackmailed," said Lili. "As a matter of fact, he never said anything about it. I deduced it."

"From what?"

"Why, from his contract with Ugbrook, of course. Perhaps you didn't know about it. D'you know how much John paid Ugbrook for that book, *Mind in Unmaking?* Fifteen hundred pounds. And there was even a clause in the contract about the amount of advertising the book had to get. I expect you've seen how it's been splashed in the press. But I've been told that a book like that is doing quite well if it sells two hundred copies. So what explanation is there except that Ugbrook had got a hold on John? That's what I believe, at any rate. I believe Ugbrook was bleeding John because of something he knew about him——"

"But how did you know about the letter?" Leora broke in excitedly. "If John didn't tell you he was being blackmailed, why did he show you a letter that gave it away? Or didn't he show you the letter? Perhaps you read it by telepathy—if there ever was a letter, which I don't believe. In fact, I don't believe one word you've been telling us!"

"Leora!" hissed Mrs. Werth.

Giving a little nervous titter, Leora went on: "I don't believe it for two simple reasons. First, John never did anything one could blackmail him for. Second, Jules Ugbrook isn't the sort of man you're trying to make him out. He's not a blackmailer; he's a very good man with a very brilliant mind, and the reason John gave him all that money was simply that John believed in him."

"Leora!" A shrunken figure, taut with anger, Mrs. Werth pattered across the room and stood over her daughter. "Leora, have I or have I not told you what sort of man Ugbrook is? Did I or did I not see fit to turn him out of my house? You know I've not often done that. You know I'm not narrow-minded; I'm interested in human nature and I like all sorts of people. But Ugbrook was more than I could stand. From the moment he arrived he was inconsiderate, noisy, and dirty. Dirty!" She threw up her hands.

"Lots of saints have been dirty," said Leora stormily.

"But they didn't go in for blackmail, my dear."

"Nor did Jules!" cried Leora. "That's what I've been telling you. He isn't a blackmailer. It's Lili who's a liar."

"Come to think of it," said Toby, who had been fiddling with the knobs of the safe, "the letter that brought Ugbrook here wasn't couched in terms one would use to a blackmailer."

Lili merely shrugged once more.

Mrs. Werth asked: "What letter? When did you see it?"

"I saw it in Ugbrook's room," said Toby. "I suppose he'd had it in a pocket, and he'd used it as a spill for lighting a cigarette. John had asked him to come here because, as John put it, he needed the help of someone he could trust. And I've yet to meet the man who trusted a blackmailer."

"Wait a moment," said Mrs. Werth. "You say he'd used it as a spill for lighting a cigarette? Well, was it, by any chance, the *date* of the letter that had been burned off?"

Toby hesitated an instant, then he nodded. Just then the door opened; Mrs. Tomlinson, entering, said that Sir Wilfred Ridden had called.

On hearing this, Toby and Constance immediately showed the same impulse to consider Lili's feelings and left the room as rapidly as they could. They went out into the garden, and after a few minutes Leora joined them. Muffled in their coats, they walked up and down for a while. At first they did not talk, but presently Constance started chatting to Leora, asking how Billy was and what Leora was doing with herself these days.

Leora replied that she was doing some social work at the North London Settlement. For some minutes Constance tried to draw the girl out about her work, but Leora gave mostly monosyllabic answers, while her face grew more sullen than ever. Constance soon gave it up, and the three of them walked up and down in silence.

Suddenly Leora burst out: "Did *you* believe it?"

"Lili's story about the blackmail?" asked Constance. "I don't know."

"Lili's always been an awful liar," said Leora. "You know she's supposed to be Hungarian and used to call herself Dános. Well, after he'd married her John found out she was really called Lily Brown and that she came from Manchester. She just made up the other name so's to sound more glamorous. But when she gets excited she forgets to talk her lovely theatrical English and pure Lancashire comes out. John was awfully upset about it. He came and told Mother all about it, and she held his hand as usual and told him he must try and be understanding because Lili only made up fantasies because she'd had such an unhappy life. She's mad about Lili, you know, simply because Lili's musical—or pretends she is. It was really Mother who arranged for John and Lili to marry. The moment you went away, Constance, she started pushing them together. Billy and I said straight away it was obvious what'd happen. John was always so easy to push around——"

"Leora, please!" said Constance.

"Sorry," said Leora abruptly.

Once more they walked along in silence.

After a few minutes Leora suddenly turned on her heel and left them. She had a round-shouldered, scuttling walk, as if she were perpetually attempting to dodge observation.

Constance, looking after her as she hurried toward the house, murmured: "Oh dear, I suppose she's upset because I stopped her talking. That child's too sensitive to live."

"And not without a certain spitefulness in her nature," said Toby.

"She's always been too much at home," said Constance. "Mrs. Werth's always struck me as the sort of mother who'd sooner eat her young than let them stray into danger. But you know, I can't stand much more of this talk, talk, talk about John."

"But do you agree with her?" asked Toby.

"That Lili was lying? Why? Do you?"

"Evidence is lacking either way."

"You know, blackmail does explain that contract," said Constance. "It explains more than one puzzling feature about it. You see, one thing I've been wondering about is why, if John simply believed in Ugbrook and wanted to help him, he had to give him a contract instead of helping him with his own money. That'd have been much more like John. I can easily imagine him losing his head about Ugbrook as a man, and even as a thinker, and wanting to pour gold into his lap. But I can't believe he could ever lose his head so completely that he'd start thinking Ugbrook was a commercial proposition and be ready to squander the firm's money on him.

But suppose Ugbrook forced John to pay with the firm's check and to give him that contract. It'd be safer for a blackmailer, wouldn't it, to be paid like that than to receive large sums from a private individual? Besides, publication and publicity may have been what Ugbrook wanted almost more than the money."

"Umm," said Toby, "yes. But there's still the question of the letter I found in Ugbrook's room—the letter that wasn't written to a blackmailer."

"But you said just now the date had been burned off. It may have been written months ago, before Ugbrook had started the blackmailing."

"That letter was in almost the same words as the letters John wrote to you and me. Did he write those letters also months ago? No . . ." Toby shook his head. "I think we're trying to go too fast, Constance."

10

Later in the morning Inspector Rogers came to tell
them that the inquest would be held the following afternoon. He spent a considerable time with Lili and Mrs.
Werth. Toby and Constance drove into Mallowby for
lunch. Toby booked himself a room for the night at the
White Horse, but Constance insisted on returning to
London.

"I'll be back tomorrow afternoon," she said, "but I
want this evening on my own to do some thinking."

When she had driven away, Toby visited Mallowby's
one cinema, but, discovering that the film was one he had
seen some months before, he slid down in his seat and
made up for some of the sleep he had missed during the
night. Afterward he returned to the hotel, had a drink
in the bar, and then sought a telephone.

The number he gave was his own.

"Listen, George," he said as soon as a voice answered him, "I've got involved in something here, and I want you to come down. Come in the morning if you can manage it, but at the latest be here by three-thirty. You can get here by bus, probably from King's Cross. I'm staying at the White Horse in Mallowby, and there's a bus stop right outside—but mind you don't take a bus that gets you here later than three-thirty, because that's the time of the inquest."

"Lorlumme," came the reply, "did you say inquest?"

"That's what I said," said Toby. "And I want you down here. I'd like to get your angle."

"Then you can want. I ain't comin'."

"Look here, George——"

"I ain't comin', Tobe. Ever since you come into my life I found meself engulfed in crime. By the way, I suppose it *is* a crime, eh?—because if it's just someone you run down and killed with that car of yours, of course I'd look at it differently."

"It's a crime, George."

"Then I ain't comin'."

"George——"

"No, Tobe. I been doin' me honest best to sever all connection with crime, and the time's come when I see I got to take a firm line with you. I ain't comin'."

There was a click and the line went dead. Swearing, Toby left the telephone booth, returned to the bar, had another drink, then went to the dining room, where he ate thoughtfully through the five very solid courses supplied by the White Horse. After dinner he went back to the bar.

He was sitting there morosely drawing daisies round the edges of an envelope when Sir Wilfred Ridden, looking rather like a seedy Viking with his straw-colored hair and beetling golden eyebrows, came in through the revolving door.

It was easy to see that the White Horse was not the first call Sir Wilfred had made that evening. He seemed glad to see Toby; he had a load on his mind, and the load of drink he had already taken on had made him hungry for sympathy. Already over his second pint he started confiding.

"This business has got on my nerves pretty badly, I can tell you," he said. "Poor old John. In the midst of life, and all that, eh? I keep remembering the things we said yesterday—ordinary, damn things like all of us say to each other all the time—and I can't get it out of my head that any time one says that sort of thing to anybody he may go and die. You, me, anybody. Just go and die in the night. Jove, it's given me a jolt. I had an aunt Selina when I was a kid—she drank a bottle of disinfectant and died. Jove, that was a jolt too. D'you know what I nearly did as a result of it? I nearly went into the church. Sometimes I've wished I'd gone through with it, too. You mightn't think it, but I'm a serious chap. Oh yes, I take life and all that damn seriously."

"You must have been relieved, however," said Toby, "to know it wasn't Mrs. Lestarke-Toye's blood on the carpet."

"Jove, yes!" But as he said it Ridden's pale, red-veined eyes slid round to snatch a quick glance at Toby. "Poor girl. Poor girl. She's wonderful, isn't she?"

"Yes," said Toby, "wonderful."

"I tell you what, Dyke," said Ridden earnestly, "I think that girl's wonderful. Yes." Most of the contents of a third tankard went down his long, stringy throat. "I keep thinking of how she looked this morning. I like women to be like that, so sort of . . ."

"So controlled," said Toby.

"That's right, that's right."

"And yet so full of feeling."

"You've hit it exactly!" Ridden put out a large hand and gripped one of Toby's. "You know, I can't tell you what it's meant to me, knowing a woman like that. Don't get wrong ideas about it, mind you. Don't get wrong ideas, old man—don't listen to what people say. It's all absolutely on the up and up between her and me. That doesn't mean I don't worship the ground she walks on. I'll be honest with you, old friend—I do. Who wouldn't? She's the most wonderful woman I ever met. But don't listen to what the fools around here say, because it's not true. No, not a word of it." His oiled blue eyes gazed into Toby's. "Pure and beautiful relationship— that's what it is. Most wonderful and pure and beautiful thing I've ever known in my life."

"Have another drink," said Toby.

"Thanks," said Ridden. A moment later he went on: "Pure and beautiful . . . pure and beautiful . . . Thanks, old man—I mean thanks for understanding.

Jove, I'm glad I ran into you. I've been needing someone to talk to. I suppose we all need someone to confide
in. That's why Lili came to me; she needed someone to
confide in, and John—mind, don't think I'm saying anything against him, because I'd a very high opinion of
old John—but if you want my absolutely honest opinion,
I don't think John really understood her. Not *really*,
mind you. I don't mean things were like they were with
her first husband—God, what a brute that man must've
been!—but just that somehow . . . Well, you're an
understanding chap yourself; you know what I mean.
Daresay some of it was even her own fault, because
she's very reserved—oh, very sensitive and reserved indeed—so perhaps John never realized how much she
needed to talk to somebody. She told me she'd never
described her first husband's death to a living soul.
Think of that, Dyke! Think of seeing your husband
killed in a railway accident and keeping all that bottled
up inside you because you couldn't bear to recall it.
Think of it! Jove, it must have been worse than Aunt
Selina drinking disinfectant!"

As Toby nodded Ridden leaned forward and prodded
him with a long forefinger. "I could tell you what disinfectant, only mustn't advertise. Advertising's vulgar."
He lurched suddenly to his feet. He sucked the last few
drops out of his glass then started for the door. Though
his eyes focused vaguely, he walked with the dignity
of a man who is used to carrying his drink, and before
vanishing through the revolving door he managed to
toss Toby his usual breezy greeting.

After a moment Toby turned to the barmaid. Pushing his glass toward her, he said: "I suppose Sir Wilfred's a pretty rich man, isn't he?"

"He's got enough," she replied. "They say he's worth ten thousand a year or thereabouts."

"And a title as well," said Toby. "Yes, I think one can call that enough. Enough for almost any woman." Thoughtfully he added: "Yet one must beware of prejudice. His mother may have loved him for himself, so why not others? Yes indeed—why not others?"

However, as the barmaid began to look at him as if she thought he was not carrying his drink as well as Sir Wilfred, Toby changed the subject and after a short while said good night and went upstairs to his room. It was a frigid hotel bedroom with no fire in it and with drafts whistling from ill-fitting doors and windows. He would certainly have been far more comfortable if he had followed Constance's example and returned to London for the night.

But Toby did not return to London until after the inquest on the death of John Lestarke-Toye, an inquest at which a verdict of "death from natural causes" was returned. There was anticlimax in the air. It was as if everyone concerned had been keyed up for something else. But no signs of violence had been detected on the body, and the medical evidence was definite. Little other evidence was taken, and the reporter from the Mallowby *Advertiser* put away his notebook with a look of boredom.

As they were all leaving the building Toby heard

Mrs. Werth's anxious voice at his elbow: "Tell me, Toby —you know all about these things—why are they keeping back so much?"

He shook his head uncertainly. "I suppose none of it's relevant to the one point they wanted to establish today."

"And that was?"

"Plainly and simply, why John died."

"I don't like it," said the hump-shouldered little woman, hurrying along at his side. "I feel there's something very nasty in the wind. And I feel you know what it is. Toby"—she jogged him in the ribs—"you do know what it is, don't you?"

"No, Mrs. Werth."

"I think you do."

"I'm sorry," he said, "I don't."

Her face puckered frowningly. "That inspector and you—you're both holding back all sorts of things. I suppose it hasn't occurred to you that that's rather unkind to Lili. Only you never liked Lili, did you, Toby? You thought John ought to have married Constance."

"Not my affair, in any case," he answered.

Her black eyes gleamed satirically. "Why are we all so hypocritical about our passion for interfering in other people's affairs, I wonder?"

"Are we?"

"Mind you," she said, "I knew they'd never marry. I could see that from the first. And I knew it was best that they shouldn't. It was an unbalanced relationship, very bad for both of them. Toby"—she jogged him in the ribs again—"*you* aren't in love with Constance, are you?"

"Not that I know of, Mrs. Werth."

"Good," she said.

"Why good?"

"Because I don't trust her. I never did. Those quiet people with the habit of domination—they're a dangerous type. But I don't suppose you'll believe me. Now tell me, Toby—you *must* tell me—what are they keeping back?"

"But I really don't know, Mrs. Werth."

One of her hands shot out and grabbed his sleeve. "You do know. You know if someone was killed in that room last night—and if it was John who killed him."

He saw how haggard her face was. "Are you afraid that it was, or—that it wasn't?"

"Oh, why do you dodge every question I ask you? *Is* that what happened? Or is it, at any rate, what the police think happened? Sir Wilfred says it's what they think. Is it, Toby?"

"Don't you know that you can't assume a murder unless you've a body to match up with it, as it were?" said Toby.

Her hand dropped to her side. Her voice was furious. "All right, don't tell me then! But you've no heart, Toby Dyke—you've no heart at all. You're resentful because John married without your approval, and you're taking your revenge on Lili now. You might help to save her from a terrible shock."

"I think she takes shocks pretty well," said Toby.

"That's because you don't understand her. She's stunned, but when that wears off she'll suffer terribly. I won't forgive you this, Toby. You're very hard and unfeeling."

"But truly, Mrs. Werth, the police haven't told me anything to speak of."

She muttered something impatiently. As she hurried away Toby turned to look for Constance. He had seen her at the inquest but had had no chance to talk to her. Now Constance and her car were gone.

Toby collected his car from the garage of the White Horse, paid his bill, and through the dusk into which the short winter afternoon was already fading set off toward London. He was living at that time in a flat near Regent's Park. As he drove up he saw that there were lights in the sitting-room window, and as he went up the stairs he encountered other signs of the occupancy of his friend George, generally of no fixed abode. Down the staircase toward him undulated, sweet and lush, the complex harmonies of a cinema organ. Toby grimaced, and the first thing he did on entering the flat was to stride into the sitting room and switch off the radio.

George, roused by the sudden silence, stirred on the sofa and looked up.

" 'Lo," he grunted. "Had a nice inquest?"

"Why the hell d'you spend all your time listening to that bloody instrument?" Toby demanded, thumping his suitcase down.

George sat up. He ran a plump hand through his yellow hair. He was a short man, dimpled and rosy, with features as plastic and vague as if they had been formed out of rubber sponge.

"I dunno, Tobe—I suppose I'm simply one of the sort of blokes who got the habit," he said. "We're said to be in a majority."

Toby pulled a chair up close to the gas fire. "Why didn't you come to Mallowby like I asked?"

"Because of why I told you," said George.

Toby snorted.

"I'll get you a cup of tea if you like," George suggested. "You look cold."

"That's probably the real reason why you didn't come; it was too damn cold for you to stir outside," said Toby. "You're getting too lazy to live."

"Well, I'll get you a cup of tea if you like."

Toby only snorted again. George got off the sofa and disappeared into the kitchen. Toby, his hands warmer, pushed back his chair a little, stretched out his feet to the fire, and started to read an evening paper he had bought. Through the door which George had left ajar Toby could hear him crooning the same tune as had billowed out of the cinema organ, and a rattle of cups and saucers.

A moment later George, in the kitchen, heard Toby's exclamation.

George looked into the sitting room. Toby excitedly thrust the paper toward him. A small paragraph at the foot of a page stated that the body of a middle-aged man, which had been found on Wednesday evening in a byroad near Welwyn Garden City, had been identified as that of Jules Porter Ugbrook.

11

TOBY WAS EATING SAUSAGES the next morning when the bell rang. The man whom George showed into the room was a burly individual with a square face and brown, rubbery skin, a square, heavy body, and square-tipped, heavy hands. Standing in the doorway, pulling his features into a bunch with one hand and speaking through the fingers in a voice so muffled by them that it sounded as if he were suffering from a dreadful cold, this individual said: "Morning, Mr. Dyke. Seems a long time since I've seen you."

"Well, well," said Toby, "so they've brought you in on it. Come in and sit down. What about some coffee?"

"Thanks, I don't mind," said Detective Inspector Cust through his fingers. He sat down opposite Toby. George disappeared into the kitchen. Cust went on: "I'm sorry to disturb you so early, but I'm afraid I'll have to ask you some questions."

"You don't surprise me." Toby filled a cup and pushed it across the table toward the inspector. "First of all, and purely as a matter of formality, you want to ask me where I was on Wednesday evening when Jules Porter Ugbrook was being murdered."

"Ahem—I see you read the papers." Cust put three lumps of sugar into the cup of coffee. "Yes, Mr. Dyke, that's more or less what I was about to ask you."

"I take it he *was* murdered? In the paper there was nothing about the cause of death," said Toby.

"The cause of death was a bullet in the right lung," said the inspector. "The wound could not have been self-inflicted."

"That's a nice, long-winded way of saying murder," said Toby.

"Not at all, Mr. Dyke," said Cust. "For all we know, the shooting may have been an accident. I always attempt to approach problems like this with an open mind. Now and then, of course, I do allow myself to form a hypothesis somewhat in advance of the facts, but that, I believe, is a quite accredited scientific method."

"All right, all right," said Toby. "Well, what's the period of time you want me to account for?"

"Approximately from six-fifteen until half-past nine," said Cust.

"The end part of that you probably know already," said Toby. "I gave Rogers the facts. I got to Redvers just after nine. If you want to check that, ask an old man called Hogben who lives in a cottage at the bottom of Hanger Hill; I asked him the way. From about eight till nine I was on my way down from London. Before that I was having dinner with a man called Sedley who's a reporter for the Universal News Service. I think it was just about six o'clock when I met him; we had a drink at the Wheatsheaf and then dinner at Bertorelli's. We'd been going to meet at seven, but when I got Toye's invitation I got Sedley to change the time. Toye wanted me to go down to Redvers for dinner, but I didn't want to put Sedley off altogether, so I telephoned Toye I'd be down about nine. Does that cover what you want to know?"

"Yes, Mr. Dyke—thank you. May I have Mr. Sedley's address?" Cust noted it down. Then he sighed. "Pity we can't get straight like that with everyone. For instance, there's the matter of Miss Crane's alibi . . ." Bunching up his features in one hand again, he stared at Toby lugubriously through his fingers.

"What's the matter with her alibi?" asked Toby.

"Several things," said Cust in muffled tones. "But that isn't everything. The fact is, Mr. Dyke, she appears to have disappeared."

Toby put down his cup so that coffee slopped over into the saucer.

Cust went on: "Her maid, who doesn't live in, arrived at eight-thirty as usual and found the place empty. Miss Crane seems to have got up early, made herself some breakfast, taken a suitcase, and gone."

"By car?"

"Well, her car's gone too."

Toby burst out: "What a fool—what a blithering fool! What are you going to do about it?"

"I haven't much choice," said Cust. "We're giving it out on the wireless that we're anxious to question her."

"In connection with the death of J. Porter Ugbrook?"

"That's right."

"But that's practically saddling her with an accusation of murder."

"There'll be no mention of a murder," said Cust.

"That's the way it'll be taken, nevertheless."

"I can't help it," said Cust. "She oughtn't to have run away. All we want is to question her."

"I know, I know. Look here"—Toby leaned forward over the table—"don't do anything about it until this afternoon. You can leave it that long, can't you?"

"Why not until this afternoon, Mr. Dyke?"

"Because Toye's funeral's this afternoon. She'll be there."

"Ah, but suppose she isn't?"

"She will be."

Cust gave his head a shake.

Toby went on quickly: "She's a fool all right, but she's not such a fool as to attempt a real disappearance. I believe all she's gone away for is to think things out. She realizes she's made some stupid mistakes——"

"Ah, *you* know that, do you, Mr. Dyke?"

Toby smiled. "Miss Crane and I have been friends for years, Inspector. And I don't believe she murdered anyone."

"Myself, I have to keep an open mind," said Cust gravely. "Now I'll be frank with you, Mr. Dyke—franker than you're being with me. I'll tell you one of the 'mistakes' Miss Crane has made. Last night she told Inspector Rogers that she didn't leave home until about half-past eight, drove straight down to Mallowby, and arrived at the Lestarke-Toye house at about nine-thirty. And yet the truth, vouched for by several independent witnesses, is that at about seven-thirty Miss Crane walked into the saloon bar of the Rose and Crown, which you may have noticed on your right hand about five minutes' drive before you get to Hanger Hill, ordered whisky, and stayed for about twenty minutes. What d'you think of that?"

"I've already called her a fool, haven't I?" But Toby's fingers, grinding a cigarette into a saucer, were savagely tense. "What makes you specially interested in the period between six-fifteen and nine?"

"Simply that we know Ugbrook was alive at six-fifteen and it was just after nine when he was found dead in a turning off the Great North Road."

"Where was he? In the ditch?"

"No, just at the side of the road. The two men who found him thought he'd been run down by a car. They didn't spot the bullet wound in the darkness."

"Funny sort of place to dump a body," said Toby. "I suppose you believe he was killed at Redvers?"

"If his blood checks up with the blood on the carpet, I'd say it was a certainty," said Cust.

Toby pushed back his chair and got to his feet. "Who saw him at six-fifteen?" he asked.

"One of his neighbors. This fellow saw Ugbrook come out of his house and go into his garage. And we know that at a few minutes past six a telephone call was put through from Redvers to Ugbrook's house. The operator isn't quite certain about it, but she thinks it was a woman who did the ringing up."

"Where did Ugbrook live?"

"In Sidford Mews, off the Gray's Inn Road."

"Dr. Gayson said he thought Toye died about six o'clock," said Toby thoughtfully. Restlessly he started walking about the room. "Did Ugbrook go down to Mallowby by car?"

"We don't know yet. His neighbor only saw him go into the garage, he didn't see him drive out. And the car was in Ugbrook's garage this morning. On the other hand, if he went down by bus, the earliest he could have caught was the six-thirty from King's Cross, and nobody answering to his description traveled by that bus or the one after."

"And you think . . . ?"

"I'm not doing much thinking yet; I'm just collecting the facts."

Toby grinned sourly. "You wouldn't know what facts were worth collecting if you weren't doing some thinking. How do the other alibis stand up?"

"We haven't checked them yet," said Cust. "This is what we've been told. Mrs. Lestarke-Toye arrived at

Mrs. Werth's house in Carberry Square at six, went to a concert with her, and stayed the night. Miss Leora Werth says that after spending the afternoon at the pictures she went, as she always does on Wednesday evenings, to a social club she helps with at the North London Settlement, getting home about ten-thirty. Mr. William Werth says he spent the whole day in bed."

"And what about Sir Wilfred Ridden?"

"Well, he says he got in from a walk at about five forty-five and sat in his library until dinner was served at seven-thirty. He was alone except for a few minutes soon after seven o'clock, when his butler came in with a tray of drinks. However, as soon as the butler had gone out Sir Wilfred began to play the piano and went on playing until dinner. He says he was practicing"—Rogers looked at his notes—"the scherzo movement from the 'Sonata in F Minor' by Brahms. He says his servants will be able to verify it."

Toby whistled. "Kind of unexpected, isn't it, Sir Wilfred Ridden playing Brahms? And I wonder if he picks his servants so that they can recognize scherzo movements from sonatas in F minor. By the way, I suppose Ugbrook couldn't have reached Redvers *before* seven o'clock, could he?"

"I don't think so," said Cust.

"What about Gayson?"

Cust smiled. "You always had a suspicious mind, eh, Mr. Dyke? Dr. Gayson was in his surgery from six till seven and then stayed at home with his family until you called him out."

"I take it you know that Ridden met Lestarke-Toye while he was out on his walk," said Toby.

"Yes—and if it had been Mr. Lestarke-Toye who was murdered, and not Mr. Ugbrook," said Cust, "I daresay I'd know where to look for the murderer. There seems to be plenty of talk down Mallowby way about Sir Wilfred and Mrs. Lestarke-Toye. But Mr. Lestarke-Toye died a natural death. He died of heart failure. It wasn't he who was shot."

"He only took a bath without using any soap," said Toby.

"Ah," said Cust with a sudden gleam in his stolid eyes, "so you noticed that, did you? Did you also notice that he had purple carpet hairs up the back of his trousers? And now is there anything else you'd like me to tell you, Mr. Dyke?"

Sardonically returning the inspector's stare, Toby said: "Yes—why have you told me such a lot anyway?"

"Because on one or two occasions I could name—that Broadribb case, for instance—you've helped me in various ways," said Cust.

"Indeed? And how d'you think I'm going to help you this time?"

"We'll come to that later." Cust stood up and buttoned his coat. "Of course, if you'd care to help me right away—what about telling Miss Crane that the best thing she could do for herself would be to come and tell us the truth about Wednesday evening?"

"So that's it!" Toby gave a chuckle. "Well," he said as the inspector stood eying him gravely, "what are you waiting for? Go on—take a look round. It's a small flat and she's an average-size woman."

Cust shook his head. "I'm not saying she's here. I'm only asking you to tell her, for her own good——"

"I'm sorry—I don't know where she is any more than you do."

The corners of Cust's mouth twitched skeptically.

"Honest to God, I don't!" said Toby.

"Yet you're sure she'll be at the funeral."

"Not sure at all. I only think it's a probability."

"Ah well, if you should happen to see her," said Cust, picking up his hat, "you might tell her what I've told you. And you might mention that a man on a bicycle, whom she nearly knocked down, spotted a car with her number at about a quarter to nine about four miles this side of Welwyn Garden City."

"If I happen to see her, I'll tell her just what I think of her," said Toby.

When the inspector had gone he flung himself into a chair. His sallow face was scowling.

"Damn-fool woman and damn-fool policeman!" he fumed.

George emerged from the kitchen and started piling breakfast things together.

Toby burst out: "Look here, George, don't you think——"

"No, I *don't* think," said George. "I ain't doin' any thinking whatsoever. I don't like crime."

"Except as a figure of speech, I'm not asking you to think," said Toby coldly. "I don't believe in loading anyone with burdens beyond their powers. But if you can't listen intelligently when *I* want to do some thinking, then there's no point in my letting you go on sticking around the place. Now what's worrying me is that I believe that darned fool of an inspector's made up his mind that John and Constance between them murdered Ugbrook."

George shrugged.

Glowering, Toby went on: "John didn't die in that room where we found him. He died upstairs. He died just before having a bath. He'd run in the water and undressed, but he hadn't got into the bath. I suppose he just crashed, and someone—the police think it was Constance—found him lying dead in his room. Whoever it was dressed him up in his dinner jacket and dragged him downstairs. From the first I was inclined to think that must be what had happened, because it seemed to me there was something odd about a man running a bath and then not having it, although he did take the trouble to change for dinner. Just now the inspector told me that there were purple carpet hairs up the back of John's trousers. Well, I don't think John ever had the habit of sitting around on the floor, so he can only have picked up those hairs when he was dragged over the carpet. Dragging rather suggests a woman—someone not strong enough to carry him—and Constance was in the neighborhood at seven-thirty. Of course I know, though the police don't, that there was blood on her hand that night —oh yes, she was on the scene of the crime some time or other. If only I can get hold of her I'm going to try to persuade her to admit it. Her version of what really happened is probably the best thing to set up against the police idea of what happened—which is that John had a fight with Ugbrook and killed him; that Constance then removed the body in her car and dumped it out in the road some distance off; that John, who'd stayed behind to tidy up the signs of the struggle, began by going upstairs to change; that at that point his rotten heart went back on him, and that Constance came back and found him dead; that she then dressed him and, thinking that since he was dead anyway it couldn't harm him if he were left to take the whole responsibility himself, dragged him downstairs and planted him with the revolver to hand on the scene of the crime. Then she went away again and didn't turn up until she was fairly certain the body would have been found. And the motive the police probably believe in is the one Lili supplied them with—blackmail."

George shrugged his shoulders once more. "Didn't you tell me last night Toye died at six?" he said. "And didn't the inspector tell you just now that Ugbrook was seen alive at six-fifteen?"

Toby raised an eyebrow. "So you were listening pretty carefully all the time you were out in the kitchen. But you can't bank on that kind of estimate; it can easily be an hour wrong."

"Still, if it was like you say the police think it was," said George, "and Miss Crane and Mr. Toye done that killing between them, or anyway with her standin' by and then removin' the body, what'd be the point of her

dressin' up Mr. Toye and draggin' him downstairs again?
She'd be usin' her time a lot better if she got down quick
to cleanin' the place up or else to removin' herself as far
as possible from the district. The point of removin' the
body was to hide the signs of a murder, wasn't it? Then
why go and frame someone for a murder you're tryin'
to conceal?"

"You mean John must have been framed *before* Ugbrook's body was removed—and by a different person?"

George shrugged again. " 'Tisn't my job to mean anythin'. I ain't interested in the matter."

Although Toby swore at him, he went on stolidly with
the clearing of the table.

Toby sat and chewed one of his knuckles.

"All the same," he said presently, "that's what Cust
thinks, and it's a bad lookout for Constance."

"If I was you," said George, "I wouldn't bother with
what other people think. The thoughts of others are
hidden from us in a great cloud o' mystery."

"If my thoughts are hidden from you," said Toby,
rising swiftly, "you've a bad shock coming to you in a
moment. In just one second——"

"Here, wait a moment!" George dodged to the other
side of the table. "Why d'you waste your time like you
do? Why don't you get on and do somethin' if you want
to help your friend? If you'll take my advice, you'll take
the opportunity you got at the moment of goin' along to
Carberry Square and havin' a nice, friendly chat with
that boy Billy while his lovin' mother ain't there. Maybe
you could find out a bit more about Mrs. Lestarke-

Toye's alibi or some of the others'. Because there's somethin' you seem to be forgettin'. If your friend Miss Crane didn't do the job—and to oblige you I'm willing to assume she didn't—then there's got to be somethin' wrong with somebody else's alibi. There's got to be, see? It stands to reason. So if I was you I'd go along and have a talk with Billy, and then I'd take an interest in Miss Leora's slummin', and then I'd go back to Mallowby and find out who was listenin' while that bloke Ridden was playin' the piano."

Toby burst out laughing. "So that's what you mean by not doing any thinking!"

George picked up the tray. Stumping off to the kitchen, he muttered sulkily: "Call that thinking!"

12

FROM THE STREET Mrs. Werth's house in Carberry Square was distinguished from the other boardinghouses of the neighborhood by an absence of lace curtains in the windows and by glimpses of Van Gogh prints on the walls inside. The grimy but shapely façade of the house turned on the plane trees in the square a regard that suggested a blandly cultural interest, rather than that furtive peeping to which, through poverty either respectable or vicious, the other houses seemed addicted.

Not that Mrs. Werth was any richer than her neighbors. As the wife of Karl Werth she had never saved any money, and as his widow she had never had any money to save. For ten years she had cooked and cleaned, had doggedly declared herself fascinated by the characters of her lodgers, and had made both ends meet.

Her son Billy came to the door when Toby rang the bell. Billy was a tall, thin, stooping youth of eighteen with a pallid complexion and long, thin, flaccid hands. He had his sister's way of avoiding the eyes of the person to whom he was speaking; in him, however, this seemed to arise not, as in Leora, out of sullenness or self-consciousness, but out of satisfied absorption in himself. He was dressed in flannel trousers and an old gray pull-over that hung loose and straight on his spidery frame. The knitting at the neck of the pull-over had started to come undone, and one strand of the unraveled wool hung down over his chest. He was in bad need of a haircut.

Seeing the visitor, he looked vaguely irritated.

"Oh, hullo, Toby. I thought you were the laundry," he said.

"Sorry, Billy," said Toby. "May I come in?"

"They ought to have called yesterday," said Billy fretfully. "Mother told me to stay at home to make sure of catching them. It's on account of a bath mat they never returned last week. It's very annoying; they're most unreliable people. D'you happen to know of a good, reliable laundry, Toby?"

"I'm ignorance itself on the subject," said Toby. "Mind if I come in, Billy?"

Billy Werth frowned uncertainly. "Is it something important? I'm frightfully busy. Mother's away, you know, and I'm looking after things. I've hardly a moment to spare."

"Of course it's important," said Toby. He got a foot

in at the door. "My actions generally are—at any rate to me. By the way, how's the tummy?"

A gleam of interest appeared on the boy's face. "It's rather better, thank you. But my stomach's terribly easily upset, you know. I say, are you sure this thing you want to see me about is something really important, because I'm cooking lunch for the old party upstairs. Fortunately all the other lodgers have lunch out, except on Sundays, and the old party doesn't eat very much, but still I've got to get her something. So unless it's very important——"

"It's all right, Billy," said Toby, edging into the hall. "I'll come down and talk to you in the kitchen, and you can be getting on with your cooking." With a hand on the boy's bony shoulder Toby eased him along toward the basement stairs. "How are things these days? House nice and full?"

"Well, not very," said Billy. "There's the old party and there are the Warrens and Miss Uppman, and that's all for the moment. The Warrens are quite nice, but Miss Uppman's a very irritating woman; she's always cleaning her teeth in the bathroom and banging things about in there and making a dreadful noise. My room's just next door and I find it most disturbing. Now, Toby"—he pushed open the kitchen door—"are you absolutely sure you've got to talk to me? Please don't think I mind having you about, but you see, when I'm cooking I like to concentrate."

"I quite understand, Billy. Go ahead." Toby strolled into the kitchen.

The odor that brooded down in the depths of the old house was like a storing-up in memory of the whole rich variety of Mrs. Werth's highly flavored cooking. The kitchen was a large, dim place, with a flyblown ceiling, walls blotched by smoke, and corners full of shadows. A range of great antiquity occupied most of one wall; however, an electric cooking stove and various other modern conveniences had been installed.

Billy switched on the light and went to the larder. After a moment he emerged with a china bowl at which he sniffed thoughtfully.

"Yes, it's all right," he said, and tipped the contents of the bowl into a saucepan. "I'd forgotten about it—it's some stewed chicken left over from the other night. I think Mother got it because she thought it'd be nice and wholesome for me when I was bilious. Dreadfully extravagant of her, of course, though I know it was only an old hen she had to stew for hours. But as it happened, I couldn't look at food of any kind. All I've got to do now is warm it up. It's got vegetables and everything in it, so I don't have to bother about them either. So after all you can talk to me if you want to." Billy put the saucepan on the stove and switched on the hot plate. "I don't know why you should want to talk to me; people don't often, except that irritating Miss Uppman who makes such a noise in the bathroom. She's a teacher, and she keeps trying to make me go to evening classes of all things, just as if I hadn't more than enough to do already, besides having such a very delicate digestion that the least bit of overstrain upsets it."

"That chicken smells pretty good," said Toby.

"Of course it does," said Billy. "Mother's a marvelous cook. She spoils the lodgers. What else d'you think she gave them the night I was in bed? A gorgeous jelly. I think it was rather mean of her really, considering I wasn't up to eating anything at all."

"Definitely inconsiderate." Toby sat down in a creaking basket chair. "I say, Billy, about that night——"

"Oh, that's what you want to talk to me about!" Billy was stirring the contents of the saucepan with a wooden spoon. "I don't know anything about that night. I've told lots of people so already."

"You didn't know Lili was here?"

"I tell you, I was in bed and feeling dreadfully ill. I didn't know anything."

"You didn't hear her arriving; you didn't hear her voice in the house; she didn't come and tell you how sorry she was you weren't well?"

"You don't know much about Lili if you think she'd do that," said Billy.

"But how was it you didn't hear her?"

"Well, my room's on the second floor, you know, and unless she got into one of her tempers and started screaming, I don't see why I *should* hear her."

"Think, Billy," said Toby, leaning forward and tweaking at the strand of wool that hung down over Billy's chest, so that several additional stitches came undone. "Think—while you were lying up there in bed didn't you hear *anything* unusual?"

"No, I didn't," said Billy peevishly.

"I wonder if anyone else did," said Toby.

Billy drew away from him. "Please stop pulling at my pull-over," he said. "I don't want the whole thing to disappear. I've had it for years and I'm very fond of it."

"Would any of the lodgers have been here when Lili arrived?" asked Toby.

"Stop pulling!" said Billy. "I'm sure I don't know. Miss Uppman's away on holiday, and the Warrens were out to dinner that evening, so there was only the old party upstairs who could have known anything about it."

"What about her?" asked Toby.

"Well, I'll be taking her lunch up in a few minutes, and if you like you can come with me and ask her yourself," said Billy. "She loves having someone to talk to. Mind you, if you can't get away from her again, don't blame me."

"Thanks very much; that's very nice of you, Billy, very nice indeed." And Toby, to show his gratitude, gave one more sharp tug to the strand of wool and undid another half-dozen stitches of the precious pull-over.

But Toby's gratitude, after a first glance at the old lady who inhabited the front room on the first floor, evaporated. A quivering bundle of shawls and clinking gold bracelets, with gouty old feet in felt slippers and with stiff, ring-laden fingers held out tremblingly toward the warmth of the gas fire, she looked as if age had driven a hard bargain with her, giving her a long lease of life in exchange for her wits.

Billy, thumping the tray down on a table, said

brusquely: "Here you are, Ma—and here's somebody who wants to talk to you. That'll be nice for you, won't it? You'll like that, won't you, Ma?" Turning to Toby, he muttered: "You want to shout a bit. I'll be down in the kitchen when you've finished with her."

The old woman turned her vacant face to stare at Toby. Then she reached for a pair of spectacles that lay on the table beside her. As she put them on, Toby saw that much of the emptiness of her gaze had come from the fact that she was almost blind; as soon as she had the glasses in place her eyes focused intelligently and a pleasant animation appeared on the old face. She smiled up at him, waved him with one of her ringed hands to a chair, leaned toward him a little, and in a thin, precise voice that sounded as if it had been laid away in lavender said brightly: "I'm ninety-two!"

"That's very wonderful," said Toby as he sat down. "I can't compete."

"Of course you can't!" Behind the thick lenses her eyes beamed happily. "Now would you be so very good as to move that table a little nearer me? Then I can get on with my dinner before it gets cold. You'll forgive me for going on with it, won't you? There—thank you, that's very kind. That boy Billy isn't really very thoughtful, putting the tray down so far away. He thinks that because I can get up and downstairs very well on some days, I can move about as much as I like. But the truth is, my knees give me a very bad time sometimes, and then I like to sit still. Why aren't you having some dinner too? This chicken's really excellent. Mrs.

Werth's a splendid cook, and she looks after me so well; I assure you, if you're a new lodger here, that you couldn't find anywhere nicer. At the moment, of course, Mrs. Werth's away—something to do with the death of a dear friend. I'm not sure who, but I rather believe it was that beautiful girl who was here the other morning. Most sudden and very, very sad. So you'll understand that conditions here are not quite at their best, because though Billy's a very good boy and very helpful to his mother, he can't quite look after things as Mrs. Werth herself would. But she'll be back shortly, no doubt."

"Er, then you saw Mrs. Lestarke-Toye yesterday morning, did you?" said Toby.

"Yes indeed," said the old woman, munching her stewed chicken, "a beautiful girl—really beautiful. Nobody's told me how it happened. Perhaps it was one of those dreadful motorcycles. Very, very sad in any case."

"It wasn't she who died," Toby explained; "it was her husband."

The munching of the old jaws stopped for an instant. "Yes—yes, of course. I remember now, that's what Billy told me. Poor thing. I was married twenty-three years before I lost my husband."

"I wonder if you saw Mrs. Lestarke-Toye when she got here in the evening?" Toby asked cautiously.

"Evening? What evening would that be? I don't remember anything about an evening."

"It was Wednesday evening," said Toby. As she looked at him with an air of confusion, he added: "The evening that Billy was ill in bed, and that Mrs. Werth went to a concert, and that there was stewed chicken and jelly for dinner."

The eyes behind the thick glasses brightened. "Ah yes, of course. Wednesday evening." She chewed another mouthful. "What was it you were asking me about it?"

"I asked if you saw Mrs. Lestarke-Toye that evening or only the next morning," said Toby.

She thought. "I saw her this morning—no, I mean the next morning. I saw her on the landing when I was going to the bathroom. That's all. But I was so struck by her beauty I asked Mrs. Werth all about her."

"You're sure you didn't see her the evening before?"

"Quite sure."

"I suppose you had dinner up here by yourself?"

"Indeed no!" She gave another of her happy smiles. "That was one of my good days. My knees hardly troubled me at all. I even went for a little walk in the square in the afternoon and had dinner downstairs with Mrs. Werth."

"At what time?"

"At eight o'clock, as usual."

"And Mrs. Lestarke-Toye wasn't there?"

For the first time her face showed a gleam of suspicion at his persistence. But she shook her head.

He offered an explanation: "You see, I was trying to get in touch with Mrs. Lestarke-Toye that evening, as I'd heard of her husband's death. As you say, very, very sad. I suppose, by the way, you're quite sure she wasn't there? I mean, you aren't by any chance thinking of some other evening?"

"Certainly not. I've a perfectly clear memory of dinner that night," she said tartly. "First of all, I remember praising Mrs. Werth most particularly about the stew. Then Mrs. Werth and I were alone together, which was unusual; as a rule at least six people sit down to dinner. But Billy was in bed, and the Warrens were out visiting, and Miss Uppman is away, so there were only Mrs. Werth and I. And then I remember Mrs. Werth spoke of the concert she was going to after dinner and actually tried to persuade me to go with her, as she had Billy's ticket over. Naturally I told her that at my age one doesn't go to concerts, but I thought it very kind of her indeed to be so pressing."

"And you didn't hear or see anything of Mrs. Lestarke-Toye until next morning?"

"No, young man, I did not. Oh"—as he got to his feet—"are you going? And I was so enjoying our talk. Never mind, you must come in another time. Thank you very much for coming to talk to me; I've enjoyed it a great deal. I hope you'll come in again." She was beaming at him in gentle, aged affability as he left the room.

Down in the kitchen Toby found Billy. Grasping him by the piece of wool that dangled down his chest, he said: "Billy, how long ago did Ugbrook stay here?"

Billy tried to dodge away, but it cost him several more stitches of his pull-over.

"Billy, tell me," said Toby, "how long ago did Ugbrook stay here?"

"I don't remember," said Billy. "Why should I? He was a silly sort of man; he used to sing in his bath. I used to complain about it and say he ought to remember that I'd got the room next door, but he told me I was lucky he only sang classical music and no jazz. I told him that I'd been plagued with classical music all my life and that all I wanted was quiet, but it never did any good."

"But I thought your mother's objection to him was that he didn't have any baths," said Toby. "Didn't she turn him out because he was too dirty for her?"

Billy chuckled. "That's just what she says. You know what Mother's like; if she wants a thing she can always trot out an explanation that makes it sound all right."

"You mean she wanted to get rid of him anyway?" asked Toby with interest.

"You bet she did!"

"Any special reason, or was it just generalized dislike?"

Billy chuckled again. "Oh, she didn't dislike him at all; in fact, she was always saying how interesting he was, until she caught him kissing Leora."

"Well, well," said Toby, "this morning is certainly full of surprises." He pulled at the strand of wool. "Billy," he said earnestly, "can't you really remember when Ugbrook stayed here?"

"No, I can't!" said Billy.

"Was it six months ago, or a year, or two years? Surely there's something you can remember it by."

"Well, I suppose it's all down in the visitors' book, if you want to look at it," said Billy.

"The visitors' book! But that's perfect. Thanks, Billy —thanks an awful lot. You're being a great help."

"A help in what?" asked Billy suspiciously.

"In getting a friend of mine out of a very nasty mess —I hope," said Toby. "Where's the book?"

"Oh, I may as well go and get it for you, I suppose." Wearily Billy wandered away. His slippers made a slow slap, slap up the basement stairs as he climbed to the floor above and then a slow slap, slap as he came down again. He thrust into Toby's hands a thick book bound in a shiny black cover.

"Now I hope to goodness that's *all* you want," he said, "because I'm very busy."

With the black book open on his knees Toby settled down in the basket chair and started to make a careful study of the entries.

He found that it was almost exactly two years since Ugbrook had come to the house in Carberry Square. He appeared to have stayed a little over two months; digging paper and pencil out of a pocket, Toby made a note of the dates. Then he turned the pages and made notes of certain other dates as he came to them. The information he collected was that it was three years since John Lestarke-Toye had left Carberry Square; that about six months later a Mr. and Mrs. Snape had arrived and stayed for a month; that in the following January Ugbrook had arrived and had left again in March; that Mrs. Snape, without her husband and transformed into Lili Dános, had returned for a second visit in August of the same year and had remained at Carberry Square until the date of her second marriage.

Handing the book back to Billy, Toby said: "Well, you and your old party upstairs have given me quite a number of things to think about. By the way, what sort of man was Lili's first husband?"

Billy made a face. "He was a great hulking brute with a loud voice—an Australian, I think. He used to cut himself shaving and swear at the top of his voice——"

"—in the bathroom," said Toby. "I know. Poor old Billy. I wonder you can put up with all these trials. Why don't you walk out of the house and get yourself a job somewhere? And that goes for Leora too." He went toward the door. "You didn't mention what she thought about it when your mother turned Ugbrook out."

"Leora doesn't think," said Billy contemptuously. "I say, you can let yourself out, can't you? I'm so frightfully busy and——"

"Yes, yes," said Toby, "don't bother to come up." But in the doorway he turned to take a look at the boy's pale, self-engrossed face. There was much about it that resembled his sister's; in both there was the look of having been grown in the dark—the darkness of that airless basement kitchen. But about Leora there was something much more passionate, much more rebellious than about her brother.

"So Leora doesn't think?" Toby shook his head. A moment later, as he climbed the murky staircase toward the light, he muttered to himself: "A highly improbable statement, requiring, I think, some investigation."

13

TOBY'S INVESTIGATION of Leora's thinking took him to
the North London Settlement, where he had a longish
talk with the organizing secretary, a plump young
woman whose cool, clear eyes revealed the shrewdness
of a mind trained in charity. What she told him induced
in Toby a mood of deep abstraction. When he left the
settlement he had a scowl on his face; the foolish and
frightened lying of his acquaintances did not appear to
please him.

A penny bus ride took him to the Gray's Inn Road.
He had to ask to be directed to Sidford Mews. Its entrance was tucked away down an alley between a couple
of shops, with odors of fish-and-chips and of gasoline
from a near-by filling station following him as he turned
in at the narrow opening. Between the two rows of

little houses the ground was cobbled. Each lower story consisted of a garage, the garage doors flanking the alley with variegated squares of peeling paint. One or two of the buildings had been converted into warehouses; to judge from the smells they emitted, the goods stored there were edibles of some fishily exotic kind. The place had a dreary, grimy air, with something fetid and stagnant about it, like a ditch that has not been cleaned out.

As he advanced over the frozen cobbles Toby had no need to inquire which house had been the home of Jules Porter Ugbrook. A group of people had gathered to stare at it. Also, from some distance away, Toby recognized the broad figure occupying the doorstep as that of Detective Inspector Cust.

The inspector was just separating from some other broad, muscularly solid individuals. As they left, Cust, seeing Toby, beckoned to him and drew him inside the house.

"I kind of thought you might be turning up here sooner or later," he said. "Well, have you spoken to Miss Crane?"

"I told you, I don't know where she is any more than you do," said Toby, climbing the narrow stairs to the floor above. "But I do know one or two other things of some interest."

"Do you, now?" said Cust, following. "That's grand. And so do I."

"Which you're longing to tell me because I'm always so helpful. No good, Cust; I find your frankness a bit like that smell out there—it's on the fishy side." Toby took a look round him. They were in a small room which appeared to be a bed-sitting-room. Toby's glance roamed over open drawers, a book-strewn floor, a disheveled bed. He said after a moment: "You know, my attention isn't usually drawn by untidiness, but if this is the sort of mess Ugbrook generally lived in, I think even I should feel kind of uncomfortable in it."

"I fancy Ugbrook would feel kind of uncomfortable about it himself," said Cust somberly, "if he was alive to know it."

"You mean the place has been searched?"

Cust nodded.

"And plainly not by police methods." Looking around him, Toby strolled through the small room into the kitchen beyond.

There were only the two rooms in the flat. Both were disordered and far from clean, with dingy curtains and battered furniture that looked as if it had come from the cheapest of secondhand shops. A staleness of tinned food was in the air. In the kitchen a table had been laid with a checked cloth and places for two, but only one plate and one knife and fork had been used; it seemed to be pork and beans that had been eaten. At the other end of the table there was a typewriter and an untidy litter of papers.

"When did the search happen?" asked Toby.

"Wednesday night, I fancy," said Cust.

"Have you got any line on who did it?"

"Nothing very definite. There are some interesting

fingerprints, but they weren't made by the person who did the searching."

"You aren't letting on whose they are, I suppose?"

"As a matter of fact, they're Miss Werth's," said Cust.

One of Toby's black eyebrows shot up. "And how d'you know she wasn't the searcher?"

"Because her prints have been smudged by someone who was wearing gloves."

"And how did the searcher get in?"

"Well, there are no signs of breaking in, so it seems likely the individual used a key in the usual manner. And as to where the key came from"—Cust bunched his face up in one hand and mumbled through his fingers—"there was no latchkey on Ugbrook's body or anywhere in his luggage."

"Wait a moment—say that again!" cried Toby. "There was no key in his luggage?"

"That's what I said."

"Then the key was taken from Ugbrook by the murderer?"

"That seems probable. But mind you," said Cust, "that's just the kind of point where you can trip up. Maybe it wasn't taken from him by the murderer."

"All right," said Toby, "perhaps it wasn't. And perhaps it wasn't the person who took the key who searched this place. Is that cautious enough for you? All the same, probably it *was* the murderer who took the key *and* searched this place."

"I'm not saying it wasn't."

"And searched it on Wednesday night?"

Cust nodded.

"Have you any proof of that?"

"The woman who lives opposite saw a light on in this room at 2 A.M. that night," said Cust. "Naturally she didn't think anything of it at the time; people around here keep late hours. But later she heard that Ugbrook's body had been found round about nine o'clock, so she came and reported what she'd seen."

"Good," said Toby. He started to turn over some of the pages that littered the kitchen table. "That's all extremely satisfactory."

Cust waited for a little while Toby glanced through the untidy pages of typewriting, but presently the inspector gave a slight cough.

"I've been telling you what I know, Mr. Dyke," he said. "Now what about some of those things that you know?"

"Oh yes," said Toby. "Only I daresay you know them all already." He had arranged several pages in order according to their numbering and was reading while he spoke. "I found out this morning that both Mrs. Lestarke-Toye and Miss Werth gave you phony alibis."

"I've men out checking up on them now," said Cust.

"Well, about Miss Werth," said Toby. "I had a talk this morning with a certain Miss Palmer, who's the organizing secretary of the North London Settlement. She had a lot of very bitter things to say about voluntary workers; apparently it's their habit to turn up with a show of great enthusiasm and talk her into giving them responsible work, but as soon as they've got it they get tired of it and vanish. Miss Werth was the same as the rest of them. She arrived, was eager to work, and took on the running of a girls' club. But after three weeks she sent a short note saying she had no time to go on with it, and Miss Palmer hasn't seen her since. It's at least four months since Leora attended the club. Definitely she wasn't there on Wednesday evening."

"I wonder whether she lied because she was afraid of us—or her mother. And now what about Mrs. Lestarke-Toye's alibi?"

"She didn't have dinner at Carberry Square," said Toby.

With slight surprise he saw that Cust looked disappointed.

"Ah yes," said Cust, "I'm afraid I must have given you a wrong impression about that alibi, Mr. Dyke. Mrs. Lestarke-Toye never told me she had dinner at Carberry Square. She said she arrived there about six and stayed and talked to Mrs. Werth in the kitchen while Mrs. Werth was cooking the dinner. She stayed till eight o'clock. Seems Mrs. Werth wanted her to stay to dinner, but she wouldn't because she said she didn't think it was fair to Mrs. Werth, thrusting herself on her for a meal without any warning. So they arranged to meet after dinner and go to a concert, and Mrs. Lestarke-Toye went out and had an egg on toast at a Corner House. They met for the concert at eight forty-five and sat through it and then went back to Carberry Square. That's her story as I ought to have told it to you."

"And a pretty dubious story it sounds to me," said Toby.

"Well, I won't say I like it much myself," said Cust. "All the same, I've got to be able to show there's something wrong with it before my dislike'll do me much good. Mrs. Werth backs up the first and the last part of it, and though the waitress at the Corner House can't remember Mrs. Lestarke-Toye, she can't swear she didn't serve her. But even supposing Mrs. Lestarke-Toye didn't spend that odd three quarters of an hour at the Corner House, she couldn't have been at Mallowby murdering Ugbrook round about seven or eight o'clock if she was sitting talking to Mrs. Werth in the kitchen at Carberry Square, could she?"

"Suppose there's something wrong with that part of the story?"

"You'd have to prove both of them were lying."

Toby's gaze was still moving over the pages of typewriting.

"Mrs. Werth herself must've been there all right," he said. "She served up dinner at eight—not a cold dinner either—and a dinner has to be cooked. But she might be lying about Lili. I wonder, would she lie? She's a shrewd woman; she'd know it was dangerous. But if she had a motive . . ."

"What motive could she have?"

"She hated Ugbrook. She caught him kissing her daughter and instantly turned him out of the house. But apart from that, loyalty's pretty often a motive for lying, isn't it?"

"Loyalty to Mrs. Lestarke-Toye? You'd say she was very attached to her, then?"

"She appears to be. I say, Cust"—Toby held out the bundle of papers in his hand—"I suppose you've taken a look at these?"

Cust nodded. "Seems to be a story of some sort."

"It's the manuscript of a novel," said Toby. "And there's something very queer about it. If, instead of assuming that it was written by a middle-aged man with inflated ideas of his own intellectual and spiritual qualities and, quite possibly, a tendency to blackmail, one thought it might have been written by a very young girl with no experience of anything but with a quite acute mind and a great deal of frustrated passion in her nature, one would be justified, I think, in calling it surprisingly promising."

"As to that, I'm no judge," said Cust.

"Well, it's only an opinion, in any case, and formed in about five minutes, so don't let it influence your view of this crime." Toby replaced the sheets of typewriting on the table beside the uncovered typewriter. "And now, Inspector, I think I'd better be going. In view of some of the things you've been telling me, I don't want to miss the funeral at Mallowby. I think Miss Crane will be there, and I'm quite convinced now that it's my duty to her as a friend to urge her to come to you and tell you every single thing she knows. So good-by for the present." He gave his sudden, rather wolfish grin. "No doubt I'll be seeing you pretty soon after the funeral."

14

MALLOWBY PARISH CHURCH stood somewhat apart from the village. It was gray and squat, with a witch's hat of a steeple perched behind the parapet of the old, square, solid tower. The sky on that wintry afternoon spread icy gray overhead. In the yew-shaded churchyard the flowers on the graves had been shriveled up by the frost. The earth of the newly dug grave was yellow and stony.

Not many people had come to the church. There were only Lili, Mrs. Werth, Leora, Sir Wilfred Ridden, Mrs. Tomlinson, and Toby Dyke. In the hush before the service someone could be heard sobbing with the soft, steady sobs of one whose tears spill easily; it was Mrs. Werth, bundled up shiveringly in her shabby musquash coat. The eyes of the dead man's widow were clear and hard and thoughtful. Staring straight ahead of her, with her lips bitten and a new hollowness about her cheeks, Lili looked as if her mind were entirely taken up by some difficult calculation. Strain of some sort was telling on her, yet in that bright, brooding gaze there was something which suggested that it was not simply the shock of her loss that was weighing upon her.

The service had actually begun when Constance hurried into the church. She looked around her distractedly, then came stumbling past the others to stand between Toby and Leora. As she grasped a prayer book Toby saw how her hands were shaking. She looked haggard with sleeplessness and only half aware of what she was doing.

The parson showed only a very abstract interest in death. Out in the churchyard his face turned blue with the cold and he coughed continually. Everyone looked pinched and shrunken in the bitter air. When it was all over Toby took Constance by the arm and held her back while the others hurried away to the cars that were waiting in the road. He could feel how her arm was trembling inside her fur sleeve.

"Wait," he said in her ear. "I want to talk to you."

With a nervous glance at his face she said: "You want to know why I ran away, don't you? Well, I had to—I had to get away where I couldn't be interrupted and do some thinking. I wasn't running away. I meant to come back. It's true I almost . . . But I tell you, I wasn't running away from anything but those endless questions. As soon as I read about Ugbrook in the papers——" Her voice shook and she stopped.

"Take it quietly," said Toby. "We needn't hurry."

They stood watching the others as they got into the cars. Then Toby guided her along the path that led away round the church. She went with the docility that sometimes goes with nervous exhaustion.

After a moment she started again: "What ought I to do, Toby? For heaven's sake, tell me what I ought to do."

"Just answer a few of those questions you ran away from," he said, "and then perhaps I'll be able to tell you. And make up your mind to start trusting me, Constance."

"I never did distrust you; I simply didn't want to involve you in my own insanity," she answered. "But now, you see, I've lost my nerve."

"Since you seem to have been doing your best to put your neck in a noose, I don't wonder."

They stood still in the shelter of a gray stone buttress.

"Tell me first," said Toby, "that night I found you searching in Ugbrook's room, it was his latchkey you were looking for, wasn't it?"

Her eyes showed surprise. "Yes, it was."

"And it was also what you were looking for in John's pockets?"

"Yes."

"And before you started searching John's pockets you'd already searched Ugbrook's, hadn't you?"

She made no reply for a moment, then she said: "Yes. But how did you know that?"

"We'll come to that in a minute. Now tell me, Constance, did you find that key anywhere?"

"No," she said quickly.

"Is that the truth?"

"Yes—yes, it is! I'm ready to tell you the whole truth today, because I think I'm probably going to be arrested, and you'd better have the truth before that happens."

"Listen, Constance, if you've told me the truth about that key, if you didn't find it, if you haven't got it in your possession, if it can't be shown that you've at any time had it in your possession, then you won't be arrested."

"I don't understand," she said.

"Well, someone got hold of that key," he said, "someone who was there before you and who took it from Ugbrook's dead body. That person used it later that night to get into Ugbrook's flat, where he—or she—conducted a very thorough though messy search. D'you understand now? Unless Ugbrook parted with that key when he was alive, which is rather unlikely, then the murderer, or someone who came there after the murderer, must have taken it. So as long as it was gone when you got there, you're going to be all right. Now go on and tell me why you removed Ugbrook's body from Redvers and dumped it in a byroad near Welwyn Garden City."

She stood looking down at an ancient, half-buried headstone. She gave a sigh. "I was drunk, Toby."

He gave a sharp laugh. "Well, that's a much simpler explanation than I was expecting—and a much better one."

"It's the only way I can explain it to myself," she said. "I only had three small whiskies, but I was in an awful state of nerves to begin with, and then the cold air on top of the drink made me see everything very strangely. I don't think I really sobered up till I got back to the house later and came face to face with you and Dr. Gayson."

"You had the whiskies at the Rose and Crown at about seven-thirty?" asked Toby.

"You seem to know a lot of things I haven't told you. Yes—you see, John's invitation asked me to come to dinner, and I left London at about half-past six and I should have been at Redvers at half-past seven if it hadn't been for the fog and the ice on the roads. As it was, I'd just got as far as the Rose and Crown by then. I stopped there because . . . Well, Toby, I don't think I need to explain to you how I felt at thought of meeting John again. I hadn't realized it myself when I started off—after all, it was more than a year since I'd seen him, and I'd had lots of time to get used to the idea of his marriage— yet by the time I'd got halfway to Mallowby I was almost dizzy with nervousness. When I pulled up at that pub I was really meaning to turn my car in the space outside it and drive straight back to London. And then I thought I'd try how a drink would make me feel, so I went in . . ." She started walking on restlessly along the path. "You know, Toby, I'm not really the controlled, levelheaded person I seem to be. Sometimes I think that the fact that that's what I'm like outside makes me an even worse muddle than most people inside. When I went into that pub I was shaking—just like I was in there in the church—and I was half afraid I might be sick at any moment. The whisky made me feel better, or at any rate more confident—almost crazily, excitedly confident —and I drove on. I was at Redvers in a few minutes. And there I found——" Her voice cracked. "You know what I found, don't you?"

"More or less," he said.

"I found everything in darkness. No one came when I rang, and the front door was fastened. So I went prowling round the house until I found those french windows at the back unlatched. I'd some matches with me, so I struck one, and . . . Toby, that's what I keep seeing whenever I close my eyes! I see just what I saw in that one glimpse I had of the room before the draft blew my match out. John at the desk, and Ugbrook—only I didn't know it was Ugbrook—lying there all twisted up, with his face grinning straight up at me——"

"Steady," said Toby. "Let's take it quietly."

He waited until her breathing sounded more even again, then he went on: "Was the wireless on when you came into the room?"

"Yes."

"All right. Go on now about what you did when your match went out."

"I struck another," she said. "I managed to get across the room before it went out, and I switched on the light. And then . . . You're remembering what I told you about my nerves and the whisky, aren't you? You see, as I understood what I saw there, it seemed to me quite obvious that John was a murderer, and when I'd looked at one or two things in the pockets of the man who was lying there on the carpet I knew that it was Ugbrook who'd been killed. I looked round the room, and I saw as clear as daylight what had happened—at least I thought I was seeing as clear as daylight. Now I realize I must have been seeing nearly double. I thought that John and Ugbrook had had a fight and that John had lost his head and grabbed that revolver of his—he'd had it for years—and had shot Ugbrook, and then that he'd gone and sat down at his desk to think over what he'd done and suddenly his heart had given out. I knew about his heart, though he'd kept very quiet about it with most people. I thought that the struggle must have been too much for him and that he'd just died quietly, sitting there in the chair."

"That's what we were meant to think," said Toby.

"Was it? Well, it certainly deceived me," she said. "And that was the point where I started to act as if I were definitely crazy. I stood there thinking that my John was going to be branded as a murderer—and I also started to think how very easy it would be to bundle Ugbrook's body into my car and take it right away from Redvers. I thought I could take it away and dump it somewhere and then come back and tidy up all the mess in that room. And that, of course, shows the state of mind I was in, because I *couldn't* have tidied up the mess. I couldn't have mended the mirror and got rid of the bullet marks in the wall; I couldn't have got rid of the blood on the carpet. But details like that didn't occur to me. I simply went through Ugbrook's pockets and cleared out anything I thought might identify him——"

"What did you do with the things you took out?"

"I put them in my bag. They're in a drawer of my desk now, in my flat."

"What were they?"

She thought. "There was a fountain pen with his initials engraved on it, and a monogrammed cigarette case—a showy sort of thing with a lighter attached—some letters and a notebook. I spent a good deal of time last night reading the letters and the notebook, but the letters were mostly bills or receipts or notices of his book sent to him by a press-cutting agency. The notebook was full of great thoughts, which he seemed to have the habit of jotting down when they occurred to him."

"I wish I could see that notebook," said Toby, "but I'm afraid it's too late; you'll have to give the things to the police. Incidentally, if you removed all those things, how did they manage to identify him so quickly?"

"I think by a laundry mark on a handkerchief, which, in my state of inspiration, I neglected to remove. Oh, my mind was functioning very brilliantly indeed!" She laughed dully. "I cleared out a fountain pen and a cigarette case and a few papers, but I left the handkerchief. . . . Well, then I got hold of him by the shoulders and dragged him out. I got him into my car and drove off. I drove in the Welwyn direction because I'd vague memories of a river somewhere there, and I thought I'd dump the body into it. But I didn't do even that properly. Suddenly as I was driving along I got a fit of panic; I felt I couldn't stand one moment more of sitting there with that horrible dead thing just behind me. So I stopped the car and I heaved him out into the ditch—and, d'you know, if you wanted me to take you to the place now, I don't believe I could find it. If you told me I'd done it in the middle of the Great North Road, I shouldn't be awfully surprised. There's almost a complete blank in my mind about what happened; I just remember pushing him out and driving off. The next thing I remember at all clearly is finding myself almost back at Mallowby and suddenly thinking that when I'd gone through Ugbrook's pockets I hadn't found a latchkey. Straight away, though for a little I didn't understand why, that seemed to me awfully significant. People hardly ever leave latchkeys behind. I decided somebody must have taken it away from him, and naturally my first thought was that John had taken it. I drove back, and that's where I got my next shock, because I hadn't been thinking until then that anyone else was likely to arrive at the house. But that shock—I mean when I saw the two cars at the door—fortunately finished the job of sobering me up. My singing as I came in—it must have sounded ghastly in that house—was simply because I knew I couldn't make a natural entrance, as if I'd no reason for thinking that anything was wrong, so on purpose I made a quite fantastic one. And that's the whole story, isn't it?—the whole of it that you don't know. Or is there anything else that you want me to tell you?"

"I'd like you to tell me how long it took you to realize that perhaps it wasn't John who killed Ugbrook," said Toby.

"Oh, I don't know." She rubbed a hand across her forehead. "I don't know just when I began to sort it out.

After I'd found that John hadn't got the key and that it wasn't in Ugbrook's luggage either, I began to think that some third person might have removed it. And then you yourself—you never seemed to think that John was the murderer."

"He may be the murderer, for all I know," said Toby. "All I'm sure of is that John didn't die sitting in that chair and that if all that you've just been telling me is true——"

"It is."

"If it's all true, then someone besides yourself and John and Ugbrook was in that house before I arrived. There's the evidence of the bath water and of the carpet hairs on John's trousers, which point to his having died upstairs and having been dragged downstairs and placed in the chair. There's the absence of Ugbrook's key, and there's the fact that John was sitting there in darkness. You see, he didn't get back from his walk till after dark, so there's no question of his having switched on the wireless and sat down there to listen while it was still light. So, unless of his own choice he was sitting there in the dark, some other person must have switched off the light after John was dead. A mistake on that person's part, but it's just the sort of action people perform automatically. And yet it's possible that it was John who killed Ugbrook. He may have done it and then gone upstairs and died, and this other person may then have tried to emphasize his guilt by dragging him downstairs again to the scene of the crime. But on the whole I think John wasn't a murderer. I think his dead body was framed."

"But by whom?" she demanded. "Who could have hated John enough to do a thing like that to him?"

"Whoever it was may not have hated him at all, Constance. Someone may merely have thought that since he was dead he couldn't suffer by taking the blame."

She gazed at him silently for a moment. Then she turned away and stared at the fields which were edged by desolate, wintry woods. The scene was already fading into the early twilight.

"And now that you know what happened that night—what am I to do, Toby?"

"There's only one thing you *can* do."

"Go to the police?"

"Just that."

"But if they don't believe me?"

"I'm afraid they've too much against you for you to be able to do anything but risk that. They know you were in the neighborhood of Redvers when Ugbrook was killed and that at first you tried to conceal the fact. They've also picked up someone who saw your car near the spot where you dumped Ugbrook. Fortunately, however, that isn't really enough for them to go ahead on, particularly as I can give you an alibi for the time when Ugbrook's flat was being searched. There's also the fact that somebody, probably a woman, telephoned Ugbrook from Redvers at about six-fifteen that evening. If you can give them proof that that couldn't have been you, it'll tell a good deal in your favor."

"I can," she said at once. "I was having my tank filled at my usual garage. The man'll remember me. But, Toby, there's something else, isn't there? Surely it couldn't have been a woman who had the fight with Ugbrook. He was quite a thickset, heavy man; if I'd got into a fight with him, I shouldn't have lasted long enough to get the room into the mess it was in."

"Very well then, I think you'll be all right," said Toby. "But don't forget that even if you didn't murder Ugbrook you've broken the law pretty seriously. Your best chance of getting the police to treat you leniently over that is to help them now as much as you can. Tell them everything you've told me; rub in the fact that you searched for Ugbrook's key and couldn't find it. With luck you'll be charged with nothing worse than being drunk in charge of a car."

"I see. All right, I'll go."

"I'll come with you," he suggested.

"No," she said. "No, thank you very much, Toby. You're being very kind to me. I don't know what I'd have done if it had been anyone but you there in that room when I walked in. But all the same, I think I'll go by myself."

"Not thinking of changing your story between here and there? Because that, believe me, would be very, very foolish."

She smiled. "I'll tell them just what I've told you."

He grinned at her encouragingly. Yet as they turned and started walking back along the path between the grass-grown graves Toby had a twist to his mouth that gave his face a queer expression.

He showed no surprise at finding Detective Inspector

Cust waiting patiently at the gate. Neither did Constance; she greeted him with a sardonic offer of a lift back to his police station. Cust accepted it. Toby watched them drive away together. Then he got into his own car, turned it, and drove back to Redvers. As he turned in at the drive he saw lights in one or two windows, looking very yellow against the chill violet of the twilight. With its crazed mixture of gables and columns and those few winking lights, the house had an appearance of leering at him, as if it were waiting to spring some joke upon him.

The joke was not such a bad joke either.

When Toby walked into the room where Lili, Mrs. Werth, Leora, and Sir Wilfred Ridden were drinking tea, the urgent rush of their voices ceased abruptly. Suddenly Toby found himself the object of the fierce, calculating stare with which the widow of John Lestarke-Toye had studied the coffin containing the body of her husband, the stony hollow of his grave, and the dark, sheltering yew trees in the churchyard.

"Don't think you'll get away with it!" screamed Lili, leaping up and advancing on him. "I shall appeal! I shall see a lawyer tomorrow and appeal against it!"

"That'll be nice for the lawyer," said Toby. He turned to Mrs. Werth. "What's happened?"

She answered: "Simply that John has left his money equally divided between you, Constance, and me. He has left Lili nothing."

15

Toby walked up and down in the garden.

It was nearly dark and it was as cold as ever. But the cold was pleasanter than the kind of fires that raged indoors. Mrs. Werth's attempts at telling Lili that there would be no need for her to appeal, that she could rely on the matter being put right without going to law, that all that was necessary was for the four of them to talk the matter over quietly, had fallen on ears that had not wanted to listen.

Lili had seemed to possess what was almost a technique of working herself into a frenzy. She had shrieked and stormed. After a few minutes of it Toby had left the room. He had been walking up and down on the lawn ever since.

Sometimes he turned and looked toward the highroad,

as if he were expecting the appearance of Constance. But for most of the time he kept his gaze on the ground. A couple of deep lines had appeared between his eyes.

Now and then he caught the shrill ring of Lili's voice from the house. Once a whole sentence reached him: "Did *he* say anything just now about giving any of it back to me?" The words were followed by a high-pitched laugh, full of hysterical mockery. Toby swore viciously in the darkness.

Presently he heard the sound of steps on gravel and saw the tip of a cigarette moving toward him. Ridden's voice spoke: "Hullo, Dyke—feel like coming home with me? I'd like to talk to you."

"That'll suit me," said Toby.

"Lili's just gone to lie down," Ridden went on as they fell into step beside one another. "Poor girl, she's absolutely worn out. These highly strung people can't take shocks like the rest of us. She's got awfully delicate nerves, you know, and I must say it was a pretty rotten shock for her finding out what was in John's will. I don't imagine for a moment it's the loss of the money that's really upsetting her; it's finding out John's opinion of her, his lack of trust in her, or whatever it was. Really, considering what a lot of temperament she's got—these artistic people, they've all got it, you know—I think she's taken it remarkably well."

"Almost perfectly," Toby agreed.

They started down the path through the wood. Ridden went on talking and Toby managed an occasional reply. He asked only one question. He asked it abruptly, in the middle of something that Ridden was telling him.

"How long ago was this will made?"

"Last Tuesday," said Ridden.

"That's the same day as he wrote asking me to come down," said Toby.

"You think he meant to tell you about it?"

But Toby had lapsed into inattention. Ridden tried talking again but presently gave it up and walked on in morose silence.

On reaching the house he took Toby into a room he called the library. It was lined with bookshelves and had thick, rust-colored curtains over the windows. There was a grand piano in the shadows at one end and a roaring fire of logs in the fireplace. After the cinematic splendor of Redvers the room had a somber restfulness.

Ridden stirred up the fire, provided drinks, and settled himself in a high-backed armchair covered in brown damask. Toby roamed round the room. He looked at book titles and at the music scattered over the top of the piano. Ridden's eyes followed him with a certain amount of uneasiness.

"Nice lot of books you've got here," Toby commented.

"Jove, yes, aren't they? My grandfather collected them," said Ridden. "Not much use to a chap like me, of course, but I sort of like the look of them. I say, Dyke"—he coughed—"I take it you and Miss Crane will agree with Mrs. Werth and straighten up this wretched mix-up about the will."

"Nice piano too," said Toby.

"Yes, rather," said Ridden. "Look here, Dyke, I was just saying——"

"Play it yourself?"

"Yes, matter of fact, I do. I don't mean I'm any good at it, but—well, it gives me a lot of pleasure, and there's no one around to hear what sort of row I make."

"Except the servants."

"Oh yes, of course, the servants." Ridden laughed self-consciously. "Now about poor old John and that will. You won't think I'm butting in, will you, but——"

"I see you're rather concentrating on Brahms at the moment."

Ridden's light-colored eyes narrowed. "Yes, I like Brahms. I like all the classical johnnies. Rather too ambitious for me, I'm afraid; I make a pretty good muck of them. Still, I get to know the music that way, and then I understand it much better when I hear it. But now seriously, Dyke, I take it you and the others *are* going to put this will affair right with Lili? I know it's none of my business, and if you feel like telling me to go to hell, well, go ahead. It's just that I can't help thinking what an infernal shock the whole thing's been for the poor girl and wanting it all to be put right for her as quickly as possible."

Sipping his whisky, Toby strolled on down the length of the room. Ridden stirred restlessly. "I may as well tell you," he said, raising his voice slightly, "I don't think you'd stand a chance for hanging onto the money if Lili did make an application against the will. I shouldn't think it'd be hard to show that poor old John wasn't quite in his right mind at the time of his death. I hate to say it about him now, but—well, look at the way he'd taken up that fellow Ugbrook. An absolute charlatan. John wasn't a fool, and if he'd been in his proper senses he'd have seen through the man as quickly as any of us. But instead he goes and pays him fifteen hundred for that rotten book of his, and writes him letters about how much he trusts him, and asks him down here, and——"

"Nice radiogramophone you've got here," said Toby. "I've always wanted one with one of those record-changing gadgets. I can never be bothered to hop up and down changing the records. And a nice collection of records you've got too—very, very nice."

"Dyke, look here——"

"Mind if I put one on?" asked Toby.

"Go ahead," said Ridden sulkily.

Choosing a record from the rack beside the radiogramophone, Toby put it on the turntable. As the record started he moved back a pace and stood watching and listening and sipping whisky as the music of the scherzo movement of Brahms's "Sonata in F Minor" filled the room. Behind him, after a moment, he heard Ridden swearing.

Toby turned.

"You want to know what I'm going to do about the will, is that it?" he asked vaguely.

"No, no, I'm not asking you questions about what you're going to *do*; at least I've not meant to," said Ridden hastily. "None of my business. I'm not butting in. But I was just trying to tell you——"

"That John's association with Ugbrook proves that he was out of his mind and that therefore the will isn't valid. But don't you know it was Lili herself who suggested that Ugbrook was blackmailing John? That's her own explanation of the fifteen-hundred-pound contract. Well, a man may be a fool to pay blackmail, but the courts don't yet recognize it as a sign of insanity."

"Then you're going to try to keep the money?"

"Have I said so?" Toby hitched a knee over the arm of a chair. "At the moment I haven't the least idea what I'm going to do—except that, before I do anything else, I mean to find out certain things."

"But look here, a lawsuit's such a foul thing—and bloody expensive, let me tell you. I'm sure it'd be much wiser——"

"*I'm* not going to law," said Toby. "Lili can if she wants to; that's her affair. What I'm going to do before I arrive at any decisions whatever is find out why John made a new will on Tuesday, leaving his property as he did. Since I don't accept your theory that he was out of his mind, I'm assuming that he'd got some perfectly sane reason for his action. I believe that I was asked down here—and Constance too—so that he could explain that reason to us. He wrote in the letters he sent us that he wanted us to come down because he must have the help of people he could trust. To me that suggests, now that I know about the will, that the money was left to us *in trust* for—someone or something. But he died before he could explain it all to us. So, as I see it, it's my job to find out what he meant to tell us and then carry out his wishes. Of course, if I find I'm up against a blank wall, if I can't discover anything, well, then I'll think again."

"But hang it all, man, she's his wife, and she's got nothing!" Ridden heaved himself onto his feet. "You can't believe John meant to leave her nothing."

"It's certainly very improbable," said Toby, "unless, possibly, he'd recently found out something about her——"

"What the devil d'you mean?" shouted Ridden. "Are you daring to suggest she'd given him any *cause* to do this monstrous thing?"

"Not the cause you mean," said Toby dryly, "because I don't believe that with John it would operate as a cause. He was the type of man who tends to regard a wife's infidelity as a sign of his own inadequacy rather than of hers. I don't believe that if John had merely been listening to local scandal he'd have dreamed of cutting Lili out of his will."

"Take care what you're saying, damn you!"

"I'm picking my words with extreme care, believe me—as you pick your records." Toby grinned. "I like this Brahms thing, I like it a lot. Well, thanks for the drink and the talk—and the music. I'd better be getting along. Miss Crane's in conference with the police and presumably doesn't know that she's just come into a fortune. I'd like to get her angle on it."

But it was not that evening that Toby learned Constance's view of the surprising will made by John Lestarke-Toye.

On returning to Redvers he was told that Miss Crane had not yet returned, but a message had come from Detective Inspector Cust. The inspector had telephoned and had asked to speak to Toby; as Toby had not been there, Cust had left a number which he wanted Toby to ring as soon as he got in.

Toby took up the telephone and gave the number. When he heard Cust's voice he said cheerily: "Congratulate me, Inspector, I've come into a fortune—and that gives me a rather nice motive for having murdered John Lestarke-Toye myself."

Cust's slow voice replied: "Mr. Lestarke-Toye wasn't murdered. He died a natural death—the same as I hope you will yourself in time, Mr. Dyke. But now listen, there's something I've got to tell you. I've got to tell it to you because I don't want you to get me wrong and think that I wasn't treating you straight. I mean, I don't want you to think I was trying to make use of you or lead you by the nose, so to speak. Nothing was further from my thoughts. I was entirely honest with you, I spoke to you as one man to another, and——"

"Here, what the hell's all this?" Toby broke in. His heart was suddenly racing.

"I'm just telling you, Mr. Dyke, it was in all good faith and without any intention of cunning that I asked you to urge Miss Crane to come to us voluntarily and give us her evidence. I sincerely believed that the best she could do for herself, as well as for the cause of justice, was to tell us everything she knew."

"All right, it was, and I urged her, and now what about it?"

"I'm trying to make quite clear to you, Mr. Dyke, that on the evidence then in my possession——"

"Cut all that," said Toby. "What have you done with her?"

"I'm afraid Miss Crane has just been arrested for the murder of Jules Porter Ugbrook."

"But good God! Cust, you can't do that; you haven't anything against her!"

"I'm afraid we have."

"You haven't. Listen. Hasn't she told you what she did that evening? Hasn't she told you how she found him dead and shifted him? Hasn't she told you her alibi for the time of the telephone call to Ugbrook's flat? Hasn't she told you her alibi for that night—the night when Ugbrook's flat was searched? Hasn't she told you how she hunted for the key?"

"Yes, she told us all that, Mr. Dyke," said Cust. "But there's no proof, after all, that Ugbrook's flat was searched that night. Someone saw a light there, but that may only have been Miss Werth, who I've ascertained was in the habit of going there at all sorts of times, whether Ugbrook was there or not. But it was not Miss Werth who made the search; her fingerprints are all over the place, but the searcher, as I told you, wore gloves. Miss Crane may have made the search at any time between Wednesday and Friday. She returned to London on Thursday evening, didn't she?"

Toby's voice rose sharply: "But how could she have got in if she hadn't a key?"

"I'm sorry, Mr. Dyke. The key of Ugbrook's house in Sidford Mews was in Miss Crane's handbag."

16

LIKE A WARM, MOIST CLOUD, eddying in formless swirls of sound, the music of a cinema organ billowed through the room where George, lying on his back on the sofa with an evening paper fluttering gently with the rising and falling of his stomach, was pleasantly drowsing.

The choking vapor of harmony seeped into every cranny in the room, filling it almost to bursting. Toby, striding in with a face of black rage, performed an act of violence on the wireless set.

George muttered a yawning protest: "Why d'you want to do that? That's Stevie O'Donnell playin'; he's a great virtuosity."

Toby swore. He tore off gloves and coat and hurled them onto the sofa.

"They've arrested Constance," he said.

"Lumme—what for?"

"What for? Good God Almighty, he asks what for! For murder, that's what for!" Toby flung himself into a chair. "They've arrested her for the murder of Jules Porter Ugbrook, and you lie there listening to Stevie O'Donnell and saying lumme!"

"Would you like a cup o' tea?" asked George sympathetically.

"Tea! You talk about *tea* when——"

"Well, if you care to go out again, there's time for a quick one before they close, or if you gave me some money I could slip across and bring something home."

"Listen, I don't want tea, I don't want anything. I want to think this thing out. That's all. I just want to sit and think. I've got to get my teeth into this problem. It's something worse than I thought. I've got to tear it apart. I've got to find the mistake somebody's bound to have made—they always make a mistake—and I've got to get Constance clear." He pressed his knuckles against his temples. "God, the fool that woman was, telling me she hadn't got the key, hadn't ever seen the key—and the fool I was to believe her!"

George shook his head. "Oh no, you ain't a fool, Tobe. I've heard someone—can't just remember who it was—say you was quite a brilliant bloke in your way."

"You stay quiet!" snarled Toby. "You stay quiet and listen. That's what I let you stick around for; it helps me to get my ideas straight if I can go over them with someone. That's what I'm going to do now. I'm going to go over the whole thing from the beginning and see if that doesn't show up something somewhere that'll give me the hold I need to start prizing the business open. You just sit and listen carefully, and if there's anything you can't understand, say so. You may be able to give me some quite useful hint, for all you know. And—well, I suppose you may as well get that tea first; we'll want it before we're finished."

Before they finished George had made tea twice and Toby had gone over the whole story three times. While Toby talked George sat cross-legged on the sofa and listened unresponsively. He asked no questions. He did not even inquire when Toby wanted more tea; he merely supplied it. Toby had talked himself past his first clarity into a confusion of weariness when George, clearing his throat, made his first comment.

"I take it, Tobe, you're absolutely sure in your own mind that this Miss Crane never had nothin' to do with it?"

"Have I said so? I tell you, I'm not sure of anything," said Toby.

"She'd a motive of sorts, wouldn't you say?"

"You mean she was afraid that Ugbrook, through his hold on John, was going to go on bleeding the firm? But she could have put a stop to that without murder."

"That's right—you can always put a stop to blackmail without murder—if you've the courage. And if this Mr. Toye hadn't got the courage . . . Well, she loved him a good deal, didn't she? Maybe she didn't want him to be exposed any more than he did himself."

Toby said restively: "I don't believe in this idea of

blackmail. Look at John's invitation to Ugbrook; it didn't sound at all the sort of letter one'd write to a blackmailer. And then there's the fact that John wasn't the kind of man who did things he'd got to be ashamed of. I know that's not evidence; it's only a feeling of mine. But I'm inclined to put a good deal of faith in it."

"Maybe we'll find some way of explainin' the letter and your private feelin's, Tobe, and still make it blackmail."

"But why?" asked Toby. "The suggestion of blackmail came from Lili, and if ever there was a bitch I wouldn't trust if she was only telling me it was a nice day, it's that girl. There was something very phony, too, about the way she made the suggestion, telling us about a letter in a safe which turned out to be empty. I don't believe there ever was a letter."

"Maybe there wasn't, and yet maybe it was blackmail. At any rate, you ain't suggested any other reason for murderin' Ugbrook."

Toby chewed at his lower lip. "At the moment," he said slowly, "I'm wondering a good deal about the exact way in which Leora Werth fits into the story."

" 'Twasn't her who searched Ugbrook's flat. And, you know, that searchin' somehow suggests blackmail to me. It looks as if someone was tryin' to get back whatever Ugbrook was holdin' over them. But it might not have been the blackmailin' of Toye. Suppose . . . suppose," said George suddenly, "Mr. Toye's death somehow made it important for somebody else to murder

Ugbrook, that somebody else bein' the person as was bein' blackmailed by Ugbrook."

"I don't see why you have to give that twist to it," said Toby, frowning.

"Because otherwise it'd be sheer coincidence Mr. Toye and Ugbrook bein' dead in the same place at the same time, and coincidences ain't artistic."

"They happen, all the same."

"That's right, but they ain't no use to scientific thinkers. Now the way I look at it is this. Toye died either before or after Ugbrook——"

"Or at precisely the same time."

"Well, if that was what happened, I'd say okay, you can have your coincidence. Myself, I reckon we'll be pretty safe in sayin' he died before or after. Now if Toye died after the other bloke, I reckon he must have been involved in the murder and it was the strain of the struggle that stopped his heart. But if he died before Ugbrook, died quite naturally, like the doctor said, just from the strain of livin' in general and the supertax and havin' a wife like he had, then I reckon it was the fact that he was there dead that made it important for somebody else to murder Ugbrook. Or it might be that seein' they'd got one dead body on the premises, they thought it was a fine chance to do Ugbrook in and put the blame on a chap who was dead and couldn't suffer for it. What d'you think of that, Tobe?"

"I'm too darned tired to think at all," said Toby. "I'm going to bed."

Yawning, he got to his feet. His eyes had blue smudges

under them; a restless gleam gave them the overbrightness of fatigue. As he started for the door he saw George suddenly uncoil his legs, stand up, and slip out of the room ahead of him.

In the passage George was struggling into an overcoat.

"Hullo," said Toby; "where are you going?"

"Just goin' out to have a quiet think," said George.

"What about?"

"Ain't my thoughts my own?"

"Only so long as they aren't realized in action that gets me into a lot of trouble—which is what your quiet thinks usually come to."

"Don't you worry, Tobe," said George, "I ain't up to nothin'. I just want a walk round the park to clear my head while I think about the key—the key they found in Miss Crane's handbag. All the time you was talkin' I been sittin' there wonderin' how they ever came across the key in Miss Crane's handbag. Seems to me they wouldn't search her until after she was arrested, would they? If they was merely questionin' her they'd never make her turn out her bag. Yet they said they'd only arrested her because she'd got the key. And that don't make sense. If you ask me, there's somethin' pretty funny about that key."

"So funny it's just one hell of a joke for all concerned."

Yawning once more, Toby went into his room. He heard the click of the latch as George, slipping out, pulled the hall door shut behind him.

17

TOBY DID NOT SLEEP for some time. Once he was in bed his drowsiness left him. For a while he was near enough to sleep for his thoughts to have dissolved into fantastic images, but even these images seemed to be part of the same argument that had started up hours ago in his brain. When the telephone bell suddenly shrilled in the sitting room he felt as if there had never been a break in the long chain of question and answer.

He staggered into the sitting room. His grab at the telephone was an instinctive action to stop the infernal ringing that was cutting through his head. The voice that addressed him spoke for a full minute before he began to concentrate on what was being said. When he did begin to listen his first reply brought from the other end of the line a squeak of expostulation.

"Oh, I say, Toby, do be careful. You aren't supposed

to be obscene or blasphemous on the telephone. You'll get into trouble."

"Not as much trouble as you'll get into, Billy, when I get my hands on you. D'you know what time it is? It's a quarter to five. And it's the police you want, not me."

The thin, high voice of Billy Werth gasped in his ear: "Not the police, Toby! Oh, I say, not the police!"

"Why the hell not the police?" growled Toby. "Our police are wonderful."

"Oh, but I don't know what my mother'd say, Toby. She always says we're the only really respectable house in the square. But if we had the police in, people might think we were being raided, like the house two doors along when the all-in wrestler who lived there was having a party. Oh, I couldn't call the police."

"Then you can deal with this burglar of yours by yourself," said Toby. "I'm going back to bed."

"Wait—oh, I say, do wait a minute, Toby! Please, couldn't you come round and take a look at him?"

"Come round? Good God!"

"You see, I've got him bottled up in the bathroom, and I don't know what to do with him."

"Call the police."

"Oh, I couldn't. Suppose Mother found out that people were saying her house wasn't respectable."

"There's nothing that isn't respectable about having a burglar. In fact, it ought to help your standing in the neighborhood by showing that you're people worth burgling."

"But we aren't, Toby; we haven't a thing worth taking. Besides, they'd never believe that was the reason the police came here. Oh, I do wish you'd come over. The burglar himself told me to ring you up."

"*What?*"

"Yes. You see, when I heard him banging about, making an awful noise in the bathroom, I pounced out into the passage and locked the door on him, and he seemed to be very startled indeed and began swearing at me in quite a dreadful fashion. I just stood there very firmly and told him to be quiet, and then——"

"Wait a minute," said Toby, "wait a minute. Tell me, this burglar of yours, is he a smallish man, rather plump, with yellow hair, wearing a blue suit and——"

"Yes, yes, that's him exactly. So you're coming, aren't you?"

"No, definitely I'm not coming," said Toby. "But I'll tell you what to do. Just leave him where he is for a couple of hours. Your bathroom's not a specially comfortable place, is it? It's pretty cold and drafty? Well, just leave him there for a bit till he's feeling thoroughly sorry for himself and then let him go."

"Let him go?"

"That's what I said."

Billy thought it over for a moment. "No, I couldn't do that. He looked to me quite a dangerous sort of character. I don't think it'd be right to let him go. But I'll keep him shut up in the bathroom until you get here. So do hurry over, Toby. I've no experience in dealing with things like this."

"You don't need experience. Just use your native intelligence. He's a friend of mine, Billy. So please let him go."

"No!" cried Billy on a note of plaintive finality. "No, I couldn't."

"Hell!" muttered Toby. Slamming the telephone back on its stand, he went groaning back to his bedroom and reached for his trousers.

It was about five-thirty, bleakly cold and dark with thin snow falling, when Toby reached Carberry Square. Billy let him in. Billy was wearing a thick dressing gown over flannels and the decaying pull-over. His face looked blue and chilled, but his eyes glittered with excitement.

Toby, grim and frozen, inquired: "Haven't any of the lodgers taken an interest in your burglar, Billy?"

"The Warrens have gone away for the week end," said Billy, "and Miss Uppman's still away. Luckily the old party's slept through it. Thanks ever so much for coming, Toby. It's an awfully upsetting sort of thing to happen, isn't it?"

"Not if you'd done what I told you and simply let him go."

"But how *could* I do that?"

"Well, take me to him," said Toby sourly.

"He's still upstairs in the bathroom," said Billy. Clutching his dressing gown around him, he started up the stairs. "He's been pretty quiet since I told you you were coming. Who is he, Toby? Is he someone you got to know in the underworld?"

"I suppose you could call him that," said Toby.

"It must be very interesting knowing that sort of person. I wish you'd seen me nab him. I say, Toby, I think the detection of crime must be frightfully interesting."

"Not at half-past five in the morning."

"Don't you think so?" Billy tittered. "Here, it's this way." He stood aside to let Toby precede him along a murkily lighted passage.

Toby, vaguely remembering his way, went straight to the door at the end of the passage, while Billy pattered along behind him.

"Go on," said Billy in a tense whisper as Toby stopped. "The key's in the door. You don't mind opening it, do you? He might be violent if I went in first."

Toby was listening. There was no sound from the bathroom.

Billy breathed against his ear: "Oh, go on, go on!"

Shrugging, Toby put one hand on the door handle and the other on the key and very smoothly turned them both. He pushed gently at the door. At the same instant he side-stepped, and Billy Werth, who had been crouching behind him, both hands outstretched to thrust with all his might, lurched in at the open door and went crashing against the bathtub opposite.

When Toby switched on the light he saw that except for Billy, sitting on the floor, rubbing an elbow and bleating high-pitched, schoolboy curses, the bathroom was empty.

Toby grinned. "Sorry about the elbow, Billy. But just what made you want to lock me up in your bathroom?"

Billy said nothing. He sat there rubbing an elbow and gazing at Toby with a lowering, frightened stare.

"All right, get up," said Toby impatiently. "I haven't a violent disposition. I just want to know what made you try to lock me up in your bathroom."

There was still no answer.

"And where's George?" asked Toby.

As there was still no answer Toby advanced into the room. "I said, where's George?"

"In Leora's room," said Billy sulkily.

"Was it there you caught him, and not in here at all?"

Billy nodded.

"All right—get up," said Toby. He hauled Billy onto his feet. "And now what made you try to pen me up in here? Starting a collection or something?"

"What made you send that man nosing around here?" Billy asked defiantly.

"I didn't."

"Oh, you didn't, didn't you?" sneered Billy. "I know you did."

"Did he tell you so?"

"No, but when I slammed the door on him I told him I was going to call the police, and he started telling me I'd be sorry for it if I did, and then he said I'd better ring you up instead. So then I knew it was just more of your snooping, and I thought I'd get you here, too, and keep you till Mother came back so that you could answer for it to her. But what I don't understand"—Billy's voice rose peevishly—"is how you knew I was going to push you in here."

"Don't you? Poor old Billy. Next time don't be quite so eager to have me walk in ahead of you; just let it happen naturally. I told you half-past five in the morning's a rotten time for detecting crime." Toby gave a tug at the strand of wool hanging down Billy's chest and undid some more stitches of the pull-over. "And now let's go and find George."

Leora's room was on the same floor, near the head of the staircase. Billy slouched along to the door, turned the key, pushed the door wide open, and stood aside with a contemptuous shrug of the shoulders. Toby, taking the boy by the arm again, pushed him in ahead of him.

George was sitting by the gas fire. He was asleep in an armchair. When Toby prodded him awake he mumbled: " 'Lo, Tobe," and showed signs of dropping off again.

Toby shook him. "Here, I thought you'd got out of the habit of breaking and entering. What the devil d'you think you're doing here? Wake up and convince this poor rabbit that I'd got nothing to do with your coming nosing around."

" 'Sright," said George, yawning. "My own idea entirely."

"Hear that, Billy?"

"Yes, after you'd told him to say it," said Billy.

Toby clicked his tongue against his teeth. "Well, let's go on from there. What were you after, George?"

"The key," grunted George.

"What key? Oh—the *key!* Ugbrook's key?"

" 'Sright," said George.

"But why come looking for it here? We know where it is. The police have got it."

"That's what I wanted to make sure of. And I ain't sure, because I ain't been able to find any key."

"Wake up, man," said Toby impatiently. "Of course you've not been able to find Ugbrook's key if the police have got it."

"But if the police have got Ugbrook's key, why can't I find Miss Werth's, eh?"

"Miss Werth's?" Suddenly light dawned in Toby's eyes. "Leora's key!"

"She must've had one if she'd got the habit of goin' to Ugbrook's flat at all hours, like the inspector told you," said George. "But I can't find it anywhere."

"She's probably got it with her at Redvers."

George shook his head. "I went there first. I took the car and went down. It was quite easy to get in, and I had a good look through her bag, but there wasn't a sign of a key."

"But that kind of thing's illegal!" cried Billy.

"Be quiet!" Toby squeezed the arm in his grip. "George, that was a damn good idea you had, and I've an idea Miss Crane's going to be everlastingly grateful. But we've got to prove the thing."

"That's right," said George. "You'll have to see if Miss Werth can show you her key. Of course she'll say she never had one, at which you'll have to tell her to think twice. But a bloke like you can always make a girl think twice. And now, Tobe, if you don't mind, I'd like a word in your ear."

"All right," said Toby. "Come outside and we'll lock this lad up in here; otherwise he'll probably lock us in.

Now, now"—as Billy started to protest—"it's only for a moment, Billy. Take it quietly." He pushed Billy down into the chair that George had left. "Stay there and count a hundred and then we'll let you out—and if we don't, you can just make it two hundred." Following George out into the passage, Toby closed the door and locked it.

George walked softly along the passage until he was under the light. He fumbled through his pockets and brought out a card. He handed it to Toby.

"I found it in Miss Werth's room," he said. "I reckon it may turn out to be interestin'. She'd got it in a sort of jewel case on the top of her wardrobe. Looks as if she kept the jewel case there with some idea it was a safe place to hide it. The box was locked, but it wasn't no trouble to open. There was two rings in it, and a gold watch, and a pendant, and so on, old-fashioned stuff and not worth anythin' to speak of, but I suppose it's all she's got. And down at the bottom of the case there was this card."

The card was postmarked Australia. In a large, self-consciously ornate handwriting it was addressed to Mrs. Lestarke-Toye, c/o Mrs. Werth, at the house in Carberry Square. Something about the handwriting was vaguely familiar to Toby. He turned the card over and read:

DEAR LIL,

Good luck. Don't worry about me. I'm thinking of doing much the same thing myself, so let's call it quits. All the best. Yours,

A.

The date was in April of the previous year.

George was saying: "It sounds as if it's from some bloke Mrs. Lestarke-Toye had an affair with, saying it's all right by him if she calls it off and marries someone else, since he's considerin' doin' likewise. But in that case why should Miss Werth keep it like that in her jewel box?"

"Hmm," said Toby thoughtfully. "Where've I seen that writing? Seen it recently, too."

"D'you know anyone in Australia?"

Toby rubbed his forehead. "I'm too darned tired to think. I've seen that writing somewhere . . ."

"D'you think Miss Werth might've been keepin' the card because she thought it gave her a hold over Mrs. Lestarke-Toye? Suppose she thinks husbands still worry about what their wives got up to before they married them. Is she the kind who might like havin' a hold over somebody else?"

"I don't know," said Toby slowly, staring at the card. "Perhaps she is. But where in hell have I seen that writing?" He fell silent; then, frowning, he raised his eyes to George's.

It was as if he read there the answer at which he had been straining.

"The visitors' book!" he shouted. All tiredness had gone from his face. "The visitors' book this morning!" He grabbed George by the shoulder. "Come down; we've got to check this. We've got to look in the book and compare them, but I know that's where I saw this writing, and I know whose writing it is. Did you ask had Leora a hold over Lili? My God"—Toby plunged at the staircase—"my God, had she a hold!"

"Mind, you'll wake someone up," hissed George behind him.

But the ninety-two-year-old lady on the first floor seemed to sleep through the noise of their descent. Racing down the last flight of stairs, Toby snatched up the black visitors' book from where it lay on a table in the hall and turned the pages.

He laid the card alongside one of the entries in the book. There was no doubt about it, the swaggering handwriting on the card from Australia and that of the dashing signature: "Alfred K. Snape," were the same.

Toby's sunken eyes gleamed as he looked up. He said: "This card's from Lili's former husband, and it was written *after* Lili's marriage to John. Lili Lestarke-Toye is a bigamist."

18

THE LIGHT FALL OF SNOW in the night had left a patchy covering on roads and roofs. North of London the fields were thinly sprinkled with white and trees and hedges shone in the faint, frosty sunlight of the morning.

Toby arrived at Redvers at about eleven o'clock. He went looking for Leora. He found her alone, sitting by the great blazing fire in the Tudor dining room. She was curled up in a chair with her arms wound round her legs and her chin digging into her knees. When he came in she turned her eyes to look at him but made no other movement. Toby saw that her eyes were bloodshot and that the lids were swollen and red.

He came up to the fire.

"Hullo," he said; "where's everyone?"

"Lili's still in bed," the girl answered, "and Mother's

up there keeping her company so that she doesn't brood."

"At that rate, you look as if you could do with some company yourself," he said.

She replied stiffly: "I don't like people and I hate their company."

He leaned a shoulder against the oak mantel. "That's rather a pity on the whole."

"Why?"

"Because on a basis of untempered hatred you'll never get very far in understanding people."

"I don't want to understand them," she said. "I think they're horrible."

"And yet," he said, watching her as she sat there still in the same cramped position, "some sort of understanding is one of the qualities you need most in your job."

"I haven't got a job."

"Oh yes, you have."

Without lifting her chin from her knees she gave her head a shake.

"At any rate"—he picked the words carefully—"you've been trying to make yourself one, haven't you?"

"If you mean my social work at that foul settlement," she said, "I think it's loathsome. I think it's horrible being charitable, and pretending you're better than other people, and acting as if a world where a lot of people are hungry and miserable and a lot of other people get a tremendous kick out of being good to them was a nice, kind, Christian world. I *hate* social work. . . . All the same, I hate all the people who never even think of doing it even more than I hate the ones who do do it."

"I wasn't talking about your social work," said Toby. He waited until her eyes, which she had turned to the fire, moved to meet his once more. "After all, Leora, you went sour on that pretty quickly, didn't you?"

She frowned. "How d'you mean, went sour on it?"

"Didn't you really think anyone was going to check up on that story of social work?" he asked.

"I don't know what you mean." Her chin seemed to dig harder than ever into her knees. "I don't know what you're trying to get out of me, either, but you aren't going to succeed."

He cocked an eyebrow. "Listen, Leora, I know you never went near that girls' club after the first three weeks."

"How d'you know it?"

"Never mind that just now. I also know that instead of going there you used to go to Ugbrook's flat."

Her lips tightened.

"The police know that too," he added.

"Well?" she said.

"They're quite interested in the fact, you know."

"Then why don't they come and ask me about it themselves? Actually I don't believe they're interested in it at all. They know I didn't murder Jules."

"Murder isn't the only odd and interesting thing connected with this case," said Toby. "At least two other crimes come into it, and that's not taking into account mere falsifying of evidence. However, suppose we leave crime out of it for the moment. Suppose we consider instead your very odd and interesting venture in authorship. Leora"—he pulled a chair up and sat down—"you ought to do something about it, you know. You're promising."

He saw how she tried to show no reaction, but the color went suddenly out of her face and her breathing deepened.

He went on: "I'm not going to pretend I really read the thing and then start giving you pontifical advice about your style. I only had a few minutes; I scarcely managed a glance at it. But there were phrases here and there that caught my eye, and——"

"Stop it!" she cried. Bouncing up in the chair, she crouched in it, kneeling. "Stop it, d'you hear? I won't be patronized by anybody. It's nothing to do with you if I make a fool of myself trying to write things—and I never said you could read it either! If I found someone else's manuscript lying around I'd *never* read it, I'd never even look at it, unless they asked me to."

"Hmm—though you wouldn't stop at reading a postcard addressed to somebody else, would you?"

"What d'you mean?"

"Stop asking what I mean," he said irritably. "Since seeing that manuscript of yours I know you aren't a fool —or not very much of one. But you've got into such a habit of defense against everybody, you've got such a layer of distrust over your perceptions, that you certainly react damn foolishly to a lot of what's said to you. In a murder inquiry the issues are serious and all sorts of things get uncovered—manuscripts and postcards and false alibis and other things. The manuscript's the one really harmless thing that's come to light, which is why I began on it. However, if you don't like talking about it, we'll go on to the next thing. Your visits to Ugbrook's house in Sidford Mews . . ."

Her small, sallow face darkened. "I know what you think about those, but you're wrong, d'you hear?—you're absolutely wrong. And I don't know what right you think you've got to question me at all. I'm not going to answer anything. You can talk away as much as you like, but I shan't say a thing. I know I don't even have to answer the police and that I can consult with a lawyer if I want to, so certainly I don't have to answer an unnecessary person like you."

"All the same, you're going to answer me, Leora." He leaned forward. "It happens to be your fault that Constance was arrested last night for murder."

"Mine?"

"Yes, yours."

"You're absolutely wrong. I hadn't anything to do with it. But what does it matter anyway? She's a murderess."

"I think not, though that remains to be seen. However, the particular evidence on which she was arrested was false. It was planted on her. When Constance came to John's funeral yesterday she stood between you and me. When she was kneeling her bag was lying on her chair. You slipped your key of Ugbrook's flat into the outer pocket of the bag. Later at the police station she probably pulled out her handkerchief, and the key came with it and fell on the floor. And so she was arrested. Tell me, Leora, isn't that what happened?"

"No."

"Then where's your key now?"

"It's——" He heard her quick intake of breath. "I never had a key."

"I don't think it'd take the police long to prove-that you had," he said. "Can't you produce it?"

"I told you, I'm not going to answer any questions." She sprang out of the chair. "Constance killed Jules, and I'm glad—yes, I'm *glad* they caught her!"

"Sit down, Leora." He pushed her back. "We aren't nearly finished. Why are you so sure that Constance killed him?"

"Who else could've done it? That inspector told us that everyone else had an alibi. And she was in the neighborhood and told lies about it, and she had a motive."

"Alibis can be faked sometimes, can't they? Your own didn't stand much examination."

"But she must've done it. There's nobody else."

He sighed. "Leora, I know Ugbrook's death means more to you than to any of the others. But all the same, you really can't go planting evidence on people, and feeling virtuous about it, all because you *think* they murdered the man you were in love with."

"I wasn't in love with him!"

"All right," he said, "you weren't. But still——"

"I tell you, I wasn't in love with him!" she repeated

fiercely. "And you're wrong, absolutely wrong about my visits to his house."

He asked: "How d'you know what I think about your visits to his house?"

"Because I know what anybody'd think. But d'you know, I went there more often when he wasn't there than when he was. I—well, perhaps I did love him in a way, but simply because he was so good to me. He's the only person I ever met who understood me at all or realized what I wanted. He told me I could use the flat to write in, and that's why I went there, simply to be by myself—oh, and of course to see him sometimes and do a little clearing up for him. That's why I went there on Wednesday evening. I got there about seven o'clock and I got some supper ready for him, but he never came. I waited hours . . ." Her reddened eyes suddenly flooded with tears, but she fought them back. "I had to keep it secret at home because Mother'd have half killed me if she'd known. She saw Jules kiss me once, and she didn't understand the sort of kiss it was, and she started making up those horrid stories about his being dirty and turned him out. You see, she's always hated anything that might take Billy and me away from her. It's her way of loving a person, keeping them completely under her thumb. With us she can do it more or less by force, but with people like John and Lili she has to do it all by very clever maneuvering; that's why she's so much nicer to them than she is to us. But all the same, I know it's me and Billy she loves most, and that's why she makes our lives so miserable." The tears that had been quivering on her lashes all at once spilled down her cheeks. Twisting sideways in her chair, she buried her face against the back of it and crouched there, shuddering and weeping.

Toby gave her a minute or two to get over the worst of it. Then he said dryly: "Now let's check over a few of the things we've been talking about. First of all, you do admit that you had a key to Ugbrook's flat and that you planted that key on Constance, don't you?"

She looked up reluctantly. After a moment she said sulkily: "Yes, I did, but it was only because I was sure——"

"All right, you did. Second, you've known Ugbrook well for a number of years and you were very fond of him?"

She nodded.

"So fond of him," said Toby, "that if he'd wanted you to you'd have done something that most people would regard as an action of very questionable morality?"

"What do you—what d'you mean?"

Toby cracked his knuckles impatiently. He looked at her with a kind of puzzled pity. "I'm damned if I know what to make of you, Leora. You've done a rotten thing, and yet I can't feel it's altogether your fault. But it *was* you who showed Ugbrook that card that came to Lili from her husband in Australia, wasn't it? You did deliberately put into his hands the weapon with which he could start his blackmailing of John?"

Slowly the girl turned in her chair until she faced

him. With some surprise Toby saw a glow come into her face.

"Yes, I did," she said, and her voice rang with confidence and pride. "And you needn't think I wouldn't do it again if it was necessary. Jules needed help. He couldn't get anyone to take any notice of him. He'd tried John already, and it hadn't done any good. I'd spoken to John and asked him to give special attention to Jules' work, but all Jules got out of Banner and Crane was a printed slip saying they regretted his work wasn't any use to them. That's something I never forgave. John didn't even ask Jules to come and see him; he didn't even write him a letter; he simply told the office boy, or whoever it was, to put in that printed slip and post Jules' book back to him. And that book's something really wonderful, something really important. I knew it just couldn't be buried like that; it had got to be published. It wasn't only for Jules' sake, it was for everyone's. People had a right to be able to read it. So you needn't think I had any scruples when that postcard came to Carberry Square. Lili and John had been married a few weeks; she'd married knowing that Alfred Snape was alive, and she'd actually written and told him about her getting married, and he'd written back, telling her she needn't be afraid he'd interfere. I recognized his handwriting at once. So I kept the card and showed it to Jules. . . . Oh, you needn't look at me as if I were a psychological case or something. I knew what I was doing. I did it deliberately. I knew that now we could make John publish Jules' work, because John was so infatuated with Lili he'd never risk letting her go to prison."

Toby had not moved his eyes from her face while she was speaking. Somberly he said: "I see."

She gave a little chuckle of laughter. "Of course I didn't mean all this to be known. All the same, if it's got to be known, I'd sooner people understood the whole thing properly. After all, they might not understand how very important the issues were and that Jules didn't do it for himself but for the sake of his work and of the people who had a right to hear his message. Very few people understood Jules properly. Look at the way Lili tried to blacken him, telling us about a letter in a safe. I know she was lying, because I know he never wrote any letter. And she tried to blacken John at the same time, suggesting that it was for something in his past that he was paying, when all the time it was her own bigamy. That's gratitude, isn't it? And I'll tell you something else, Toby!" Like a spring uncoiling, Leora leaped out of her chair. "She's going to do it again. John may be dead, but Alfred Snape isn't—and yet in a few months, you'll see, she'll be married to Sir Wilfred Ridden!"

The door burst open.

With black eyes staring dazedly out of her shriveled face, Mrs. Werth stood before them. Small, humped, and rigid, she was clutching at the doorposts. Her face looked vacant with shock.

Leora shrunk back. But it was not the shock of over-hearing her daughter that Mrs. Werth had suffered.

"She's dead," she said heavily.

Leora gave a cry.

"Lying there in her bed asleep—but dead, really." Mrs. Werth let go of one of the doorposts and pressed a hand against her throat.

Toby thrust past her. He raced up the stairs.

In her room, with a heaviness of perfume in the air and the silk curtains still drawn, in the great, frilled bed with her auburn hair spread loosely over the pale green pillow, lay Lili Lestarke-Toye. One beautiful bare arm was flung out across the velvet quilt; one was crooked under her head. Her long dark eyelashes curved against her cheeks.

In a couple of strides Toby reached her side.

Her beauty, in its pallor and stillness, was to him, for the first time, very moving. He stood still, looking at her, as she lay there in the dimness of the curtained room. Small, deep lines had appeared round his eyes. He took a swift glance round the room. Nothing seemed out of order. Shrugging slightly, he turned to the bed again.

Lili's eyes were open, staring at him.

She snarled: "What the ruddy hell d'you think you're doing here?"

19

TOBY DREW BACK. "I beg your pardon," he said. "I thought you were dead."

"You mean you hoped I was," said Lili.

He smiled. "Going in for psychology? I suppose you don't happen to know who *is* dead?"

She pushed herself up on one elbow. "Get out of here!"

"Of course," he said. "Very sorry, Lili—didn't mean to wake you."

"Get out!" she hissed. She jerked herself a little higher in the bed, showing a white shoulder under a froth of chiffon. "Get out and keep out—and keep out of this house too! You aren't wanted here. And if anyone's dead, I hope it's your dear friend Constance!"

But Toby had thought of that already.

He whirled on Mrs. Werth, who had followed him. "Is it Constance?" he demanded.

"Is Constance what?" she asked.

"Is Constance dead? How did you hear it?"

"On the telephone just now from Billy. But I never said anything about its being Constance. It's poor old Adeline Bievers. Oh, think of the poor old soul dying like that all by herself."

"And who," asked Toby with restraint, "is poor old Adeline Bievers?"

"An old lady who's been lodging with me for ages—such a dear, good old soul." Mrs. Werth sat down. "I don't know why, but it's shaken me terribly. Perhaps it's the way it's come on top of everything else. I feel as if it were somebody close to me who'd died."

Lili said ironically: "He pretended he thought it was me who was dead, so he could get in and take a look at me."

Toby ground his teeth. "How did she die?" he asked.

"The way very old people usually do die—in her sleep. Oh dear," said Mrs. Werth, "if I were sensible I suppose I'd be saying it was a merciful release, but she seemed to get such a lot out of life still. . . . You know, I always let the people who live in my house mean much more to me than I ought; I always let myself get too fond of them. And though poor old Mrs. Bievers was a little childish sometimes, she was so good and kind . . ." She fumbled with a handkerchief as a tear ran down her cheek.

"I suppose she was the old party upstairs," said Toby thoughtfully.

"That's what Billy always called her." Mrs. Werth looked at him sharply. "But how did you know that?"

"I had an interesting talk with her yesterday morning," said Toby.

Something altered slightly in the way both women were looking at him.

He went on: "She told me——" But suddenly he struck one fist against the open palm of the other hand. "Good God Almighty, what a fool I am!"

"Toby!" cried Mrs. Werth. "Toby, where are you going?"

He was out on the landing already. "Telephone!" he called back.

"I told you to get out of this house!" Lili shouted after him.

"So I will, very shortly."

"Toby!" cried Mrs. Werth. "Toby, what's the matter? Whom are you going to ring up?" She came pattering after him down the stairs.

"Detective Inspector Cust," said Toby.

"But why?"

"Because I've just discovered the solution to a peculiar problem of space and time," said Toby.

He dashed into the small sitting-room and snatched up the telephone. For the next half-hour he tried to get in touch with Inspector Cust. He tried Scotland Yard, the local police station, and Cust's private address. He had to end by leaving a message asking Cust to call him.

Mrs. Werth had stood listening. Leora, too, had come into the room. When finally he put the telephone down Mrs. Werth burst out: "I insist on your telling me what you're thinking, Toby. Why did my telling you of Adeline Bievers' death make you rush to get in touch with the police?"

Toby sat back, fumbling for his cigarettes. "It oughtn't to have taken her death to make me do it," he said grimly. "I've had the fact I needed ever since yesterday morning. And that, I should think, may be an unpleasant shock for somebody."

Mrs. Werth came forward a couple of steps. "Will you answer me properly, Toby?"

He jerked a thumb at the door. "Who's that out there?"

"It's only Sir Wilfred. Please"—she wrung her hands together—"please don't be so inhuman. You know what these terrible events mean to me. Don't tell me you think that poor old thing was——"

He held out his cigarettes to her. "Well, I don't myself believe that Mrs. Bievers died naturally."

"No, no, you can't mean that," she said. "You know nothing whatever about it."

"No, but it's difficult to believe in the naturalness of a death that's so amazingly convenient."

She snatched a cigarette but did not wait for him to light it. Restlessly she started her little jerky steps up and down the room.

"Absolutely ridiculous," she said. "I don't know what's come over you. I used to think you such a shrewd, sensible person. But your mind just welters in melodrama nowadays. You'd see something suspicious in the daisies coming up in the spring. The most astonishing thing about Adeline Bievers' death is that it didn't happen ten years ago."

"Perhaps that's true," said Toby. "But two astonishing occurrences don't add up to a commonplace."

"Oh, stop being so clever! What's all this fuss about the police? Are you being stupid and callous on purpose?"

"It's just that I'm taking no chances," he said.

"You're letting yourself think in a cheap, sensational, and heartless fashion."

"Well"—he shrugged—"Mrs. Bievers' death does happen to be very convenient to a certain person, or it would be if she hadn't already spoken to me."

"What person?" She stopped her pacing a moment to stare at him.

"The person who killed Ugbrook, of course, and arranged this whole business down here. Mrs. Bievers happened to know a certain fact——"

"Why, she'd never even met Ugbrook."

"Oh, she didn't know the significance of what she knew," said Toby. "All the same, it may turn out very awkward for this person I have in mind that she had the chance to impart it to me."

"This person you have in mind . . ." Mrs. Werth came up to him and searched his face. "Is that really what you meant to say, Toby? Have you a particular person in mind?"

He nodded.

After an instant, with a slight sigh, she turned away. She knocked some ash into an ash tray. "And what are you going to do about it?" she asked.

Leora broke in: "Try to get a lot of kudos for himself by smearing it all over the papers."

"Be quiet, Leora. Toby——"

"I'll use my knowledge first to have Constance freed," he replied.

"That means taking it to the police."

"Well?"

Mrs. Werth shrugged her narrow shoulders. "Of course, if you have evidence that clears Constance, you must use it. But, Toby, surely . . . Isn't there some other way? Ugbrook was something so low, so corrupt. A swindler, a blackmailer. And punishment puts nothing right."

"Was Adeline Bievers a blackmailer? Was she low and corrupt?"

With a violent gesture Mrs. Werth flung her cigarette away.

"You're all wrong about Mrs. Bievers. There was nothing abnormal about her death. But I know you don't want to see reason; you've got to have your melodrama as some people have to have dope. I only hope the police laugh at you as you deserve. Come, Leora."

Toby remained where he was. Smoking, tugging at his long chin, he sat there for some minutes. Once or twice he looked at his watch. There was still no call from Cust.

Presently he rose abruptly and went out into the hall. In a whispering group at one end he found the two Werths, Sir Wilfred Ridden, and Lili. Lili was wearing a long blue woolen house coat; her auburn hair hung heavy and straight to her shoulders. As Toby emerged the whispering ceased abruptly; all four turned to look at him.

Toby went to the front door and out onto the steps. But before he had started to descend he heard his name called. Looking back, he saw Lili advance a few steps toward him.

It was a dramatic advance. It was slow and proud; it ought to have been made to the accompaniment of music. In the middle of the hall, posing herself carefully, she stood still, and to Toby's astonishment her face took on an expression that was easily recognizable as one of high and noble renunciation.

"If you have a moment to spare me," she said in the flat, fluty tone that sounded as if it had had some accent drilled out of it, "I have something to say to you."

Toby said: "Didn't you tell me to get out as quickly as I could?"

"I did, and I must apologize for it," said Lili. "I was forgetting this is not my house and I haven't the right to ask you to leave it."

Toby raised an eyebrow. "It's all right—I'm just going."

She lifted a hand. "Please. I said I had something to say to you. It's something"—that flat voice developed an edge—"which I've no doubt you'll be very glad to hear.

I've decided, on thinking it over, not to make any appeal against John's will."

From behind her came an exclamation. Ridden took a couple of steps to her side.

Lili went on: "I've decided to go back to my old work, the work I abandoned for John's sake. I know I shall have to start again at the bottom; it'll be hard and disappointing. But my mind's quite made up. Since John has shown what his real feelings for me were, I know I'd sooner die than accept anything from him."

Toby said dryly: "I'd take a little longer to think it over if I were you."

"I don't need any longer," said Lili. "I realize now that I altogether misunderstood my husband. I loved a man who never existed. It was for a man who never existed that I gave up my career, that I gave up success and fame and——"

"Don't leave out your art," said Toby.

Her face reddened. She forgot herself. "Why, you cheap, lousy——"

Toby shook his head. "Go on with the act, Lili. Low abuse is out of place in it."

Ridden thrust himself forward. "Another word like that, Dyke, and I'll——"

"Please," said Lili. "He's quite right, Wilfred. To descend to a quarrel with this man would be out of place in the extreme. I'm sorry I lost hold of myself for a moment."

"But, Lili——"

"Please . . . With my world in ruins, as it is, with

nothing left to me out of a life that seemed so beautiful and rich, the last thing I could bear would be vulgar wrangling."

"That's better," said Toby. "Now about John's will——"

"I've said all I have to say about it," she said. "I shall not appeal against it."

Ridden wheezed in his distress: "But, Lili, I'm sure you ought to think it over. Not that I don't sympathize with the way you feel. Jove, I know just what a knock this must mean to you, and I think it's wonderful the way you're taking it. I like your independence; I think it's grand. But I think you could easily show that John wasn't in his right mind when he made that will."

"I don't want a penny of John's!"

"But don't you see, if he wasn't in his right mind, then he didn't know what he was doing? I mean, it doesn't mean he didn't love you or anything of that sort, so there'd be nothing whatever against your taking the money."

"I don't want the money! I'm going back to where I belong; I'm going back to the life I understand and the people I understand."

Ridden's pale eyes beamed with admiration. "I think you're marvelous, Lili. But all the same, I'm sure there's a mistake somewhere."

"You're right," said Toby, "there *is* a mistake somewhere."

At his words Mrs. Werth came forward. She watched with a stare of nervous expectancy.

"The mistake, Lili," said Toby, "is in trying to make us believe that John didn't love you, wasn't loyal to you, tricked you into your great sacrifices and betrayed you. John's trouble was that he'd have done any darned thing on earth for you."

Lili looked blank. Then with hands coming up with curling fingers as if she wanted to claw at his face, she shrieked at him: "Can't you get out of here? I've told you I'm not going to contest the will. Isn't that enough for you?"

"I don't give a damn what you do about the will," said Toby. "But don't try putting it about that John's making his will like that was an act of treachery. You know why he made it like that; you know he was doing his best to protect you from the consequences of your own stupidity and dishonesty."

She drew back a little. "What d'you mean?"

"God, I get fed up with these people who keep asking one what one means when they know it as well as one does oneself! Well, I'm going. But don't forget what I've just said. It isn't going to help you to blacken John's character. He was a fool. He seems to have been lacking in sound judgment in most things. But with death waiting for him he was using his last energies to make you safe. It'll be your own fault if he didn't succeed in it." Leaving silence behind him, Toby turned, went out through the door, down the steps, and flung himself into his car. He was breathing fast; his face was excited and angry.

The excitement and anger clouded his memory. He

was halfway down the drive before he remembered why he had been on his way out of the house when Lili stopped him.

He said what he felt and stopped the car. Some rooks were flapping above the treetops; their cawing echoed sharply in the still, cold air. Toby felt for his cigarettes, but the packet, when he fumbled inside it, turned out to be empty. Crumpling it, he dropped it at his feet. Then he started to back the car up the drive again.

He pulled up a little before reaching the house. Getting out, he took a look round, then walked rapidly toward the garage. His footsteps left crisp tracks across the frozen snow. He tried the garage door. It was unlocked and slid back smoothly on its rollers. He took another look over his shoulder, then went inside and pulled the door to behind him.

In the light from a small window he inspected the car in the garage. He had started a mournful whistling, but at what he saw the whistling stopped. He gave a laugh. It was an evil sound, a snarling parody of amusement. He looked inside the car but saw nothing there that held his attention. Whistling again, he went out onto the snow-covered drive.

Skirting the house, he arrived at the back door. Mrs. Tomlinson let him in. She was wearing a hat and coat and was buttoning a pair of black cotton gloves. As Toby stepped into the kitchen he saw a battered suitcase and two or three paper parcels on the table.

"Hullo," he said. "Leaving?"

"That I am," she replied.

"Fed up?"

She gave herself an indignant shake, so that a starched petticoat rustled under her black skirt.

"That I am and no mistake. I came back to oblige and to show my respect for the memory of poor Mr. Lestarke-Toye, and not a single word of thanks have I had. Not that I want thanks for doing what I only consider my duty. We ought not to want thanks for only doing what's right. But when I'm putting myself out for other people I do expect a little consideration and appreciation. Here I am, running a house full of visitors singlehanded, and if I can't do everything just right it shouldn't be blamed on me. I'm doing my best, and that ought to do for everyone."

"Certainly it should," said Toby. "By the way, I suppose there hasn't been a telephone call for me during the last few minutes?"

"No sir."

"When the telephone rings, who usually answers it?"

"Parkes did, when he was here."

"I'm expecting a call," said Toby, "but I don't want to wait for it any longer. I wonder if you could wait for it and give a message that I'll write down for you."

"Well, I was just meaning to leave . . ."

Toby brought a ten-shilling note out of his pocket.

Mrs. Tomlinson said: "Oh, very well, sir, thank you. I'm sure I'm always glad to oblige. Whom will your telephone call be from?"

"Detective Inspector Cust," said Toby. "And here's what I want you to say." He bent over the table and wrote a few lines on a piece of paper. "Just tell him that I've gone on to London and that I left you this note and asked you to read it to him."

She took the paper. In a toneless voice, omitting all punctuation, she read aloud: " 'Please go to Mrs. Werth's house in Carberry Square where an old lady died last night her death ought to be investigated as she knew more than was good for her and as I have found frozen snow on the top of the car in Mrs. Lestarke-Toye's garage it didn't start snowing until after one last night and it stopped before six please go to Carberry Square it may be very important I will join you there and tell you the rest Toby Dyke.' " She gasped for breath. Then, as she took in the meaning of what she had just read, she stared in dismay at the paper in her hand. "Why, you don't mean——"

"That was fine," said Toby hurriedly. "Please read it just like that. And I'll be on my way. I'm exceedingly grateful. Incidentally, if you can get that message to Inspector Cust without being overheard by anyone else in the house, so much the better. Good-by, Mrs. Tomlinson."

Still staring at the paper and shaking her head, she muttered, "Good-by, sir."

"By the way," he said, "I suppose you didn't hear anything of a car starting up in the night or coming back?"

"My bedroom faces the other way; I wouldn't hear anything." Again with startled awe in her voice she began to read: " '. . . an old lady died last night . . .' "

Toby could still hear her mumbling over the message as he left the kitchen and made for his car.

He negotiated the drive and the slippery steepness of Hanger Hill, but after that he drove fast. On the long, empty stretch of slushy road before he reached the main road to London he forced his speed up as much as he dared. He did not even stop to buy cigarettes when he reached the Rose and Crown.

Had he stopped, he might have noticed something that would have put an end to his speeding. But he drove straight on, and the first he knew of the curious condition of his tires was a roar and a flash—a roar that seemed to last eternally and yet to be swallowed up instantly in a great blackness.

The cyclist whom he had passed on the road a moment before saw a car with a burst tire shooting wildly across the road, crashing a wall, and overturning.

20

So far as the car was concerned, that was the end of things. So far as Toby was concerned, it was very nearly the end of things. But all he knew of it was that after a black glimpse of eternity, consciousness suddenly returned. It returned so suddenly that it felt like a blow, which sent him reeling straight back into the blackness.

His second return, a minute or two later, lasted longer. This time he deliberately closed his eyes against the glare of the snow. Noises sang in his head and a loop of red-hot wire seemed to have been drawn tight round his brain. He found that his closed eyes were looking at a face. It was a face which, so far as he knew, he had never seen in his life, yet it was printed on his mind as distinctly as the unknown faces seen in nightmares. It was a round, ordinary face with horn-rimmed spectacles and a stare of feverish interest in the eyes. Toby realized that he was feeling very sick.

When once more he opened his eyes he saw a face above him, but not the face with the spectacles. It was reddish and freckled, with eyes of uncommonly pale blue and bristling, sandy eyebrows.

"Jove," said this face to him, "that was a near thing. Miracle, positive miracle!"

Toby tried to move his head. He heard immediately: "Now, now, old man, don't try to overdo it. Take your time. You're absolutely all right. Just take things easy and don't worry."

"What the hell happened?" asked Toby dazedly. "And what are you doing here? I thought I was almost halfway back to London."

"So you are, old boy, so you are. And so was I." Ridden laughed cheerily. "No need to worry. Everything's okay."

"But how did you get here?" Toby's head was beginning to clear. Raising it again, he managed to heave himself up onto one elbow. "Were you following me?"

"Look here, I wish you wouldn't worry about things," Ridden answered. "You've had a nasty smash but you're all right. You'll be yourself in no time, but don't hurry it. Take things easy, that's my tip, old boy."

Toby managed to turn his head. The movement made the wire round his brain jerk tighter, and a pain shot up the back of his neck. But he succeeded in seeing past Ridden to where his car lay crumpled in the ditch. He also saw over Ridden's shoulder the face he had seen a moment before, the round, commonplace face with horn-rimmed glasses. It belonged to a young man in leggings and a cycling cape.

The young man asked anxiously: "I say, are you sure you're all right?"

"Sir Wilfred seems sure," said Toby. "Did *you* see what happened?"

"Yes," said the young man, "it happened just after you'd passed me. One of your tires burst and you went slap into the wall. You got thrown out somehow."

"When did *he* turn up?"

"A few minutes later," said the cyclist. "I signaled the first couple of cars that came along. When this gentleman said he'd stay and look after you the other people went on. They——"

"What other people?"

"Now, now, old chap, don't get worked up, take things easy," said Ridden. "It was Lili and Mrs. Werth and Leora."

"On their way up to London?"

"Yes, of course. Don't you remember about the old lady, Mrs. What's-her-name, the one who died? Mrs. Werth had to go back, of course."

"Of course." But Toby swore. He had sat up. "Are you going on to London?" he asked Ridden.

"Well, I was. They all seemed rather upset, so I thought I'd go with them in case I could help in some way."

"Can you give me a lift?"

Ridden looked uncertain. "Don't you think I'd better take you back to Redvers?"

"I want to go to London," said Toby.

"Well, if you're sure that's all right . . ."

"I suppose you haven't any brandy?"

"Yes, matter of fact, I have. I say, I'm sorry, I didn't think."

"No!" barked the cyclist in spectacles. "No, certainly not. In my first-aid handbook it stresses the importance of the fact that in cases of bleeding spirits should never be administered."

"Bleeding?" Toby lifted a cautious hand and found that his head was bandaged. "All the same, I think I'd like some of that brandy."

As Ridden went to his car to fetch the brandy Toby got onto his feet. He ached acutely in several places and he felt as if it were only by his own personal effort that the scene in front of him stayed in place. There seemed a probability that if he stopped concentrating for an instant the objects he was looking at would lose their stable relationship with one another; even while he was keeping an eye on them they showed a tendency to jig up and down. He walked toward his car. Ridden, returning with a flask, found him holding onto a piece of the wreckage and concentrating on a part of it with a half-dazed frown of bewilderment on his face.

"Here you are," said Ridden. "This'll buck you up."

"They've been slashed," said Toby.

"They?"

"My tires. They've been slashed."

"Now, look here, old boy, take it easy."

"Look at them. I tell you, they've been slashed."

Ridden was unscrewing the flask. "You must've come a cropper! But you'll be all right in no time. Don't you worry."

"But look, man, look!"

"He's right," said the cyclist, who was stooping over one of the wheels, "they *have* been slashed." Suddenly he looked up at Toby with a glow of alarm behind his spectacles. "But then that accident was meant to happen!"

"You can bet your life it was," said Toby.

"But—but we must inform the police at once."

"My God!" said Ridden. "But whoever can have done a thing like that?"

Toby said casually: "Some naughty little boy, no doubt." He reached for the flask. As he drank from it his eyes sought Ridden's and he winked.

The cyclist was saying: "We must certainly tell the police. Pranks like this can be a serious menace to the safety of all."

"That's right," said Toby. The brandy had begun to clear his brain. "We must tell the police; we must tell Inspector Rogers. Now I wonder"—he looked at the cyclist—"I wonder if it would be troubling you too much to ask you to telephone to the police station and tell Inspector Rogers about my tires? It's rather important that my friend and I should get on to London."

"But won't you be required to give evidence?"

"Naturally," said Toby. "But Inspector Rogers knows all about us both and won't mind taking our evidence later. Of course, if you can't spare the time . . ." He paused hopefully.

"All right," said the young man, "I'll see to it."

"Here's my name and address," said Toby.

"But look here, Dyke," said Ridden, "I simply don't understand. Who could've done it? Your car was standing——"

Toby stopped him with a scowl. As Ridden shrugged peevishly, Toby started to thank the cyclist for his help. A few minutes later, in Ridden's car, they were on their way to London.

Ridden soon came back to his question. "Look here, Dyke——"

Closing his eyes and slumping in his seat, Toby gave a groan.

Ridden glanced at him and muttered something. It was some time before he started again: "But look here, Dyke, your car was standing outside the house all the time, wasn't it? Well, who could have got at it?"

"Anyone," said Toby.

"But——"

"Anyone in the house," said Toby. "If you're working on the assumption that it was someone from elsewhere, it isn't surprising you're puzzled."

"That's an infamous suggestion."

"Not nearly as infamous as smashing up my car."

"You mean to tell me you seriously believe that one of those ladies——"

"Or yourself," said Toby.

Ridden's jaws closed with a snap. The suburbs, dappled with snow, were closing in on them. Suddenly he said: "Concussion often has very curious effects. I imagine you're suffering from concussion."

"You have a convenient imagination," said Toby.

"Concussion," Ridden said again reassuringly, "yes, concussion." After that he seemed content to drive in silence.

By the time they reached Highgate they saw that they were driving into a fog. Though it was not very thick, a premature brownish twilight colored the air. The streets of churned-up slush looked grubbily desolate in the sulphur-tainted dusk.

Ridden drove to Carberry Square. At their ring Leora came to the door, looked indifferently at Toby's bandages, and without a word showed the two men into the sitting room. She lit the gas fire. The room was a long one with two tall windows looking out on to the square. The walls were covered by rather decayed paneling that had been painted pale yellow. Only a small space in front of the hearth was warmed by the gas fire.

Toby, whose knees still felt inclined to give under him, sat down quickly. Ridden roamed about. After a few minutes Mrs. Werth hurried in, and Lili, a cigarette dangling from her lips, stalked in after her.

"Heavens, I'm glad to see you alive, Toby," said Mrs. Werth, but there was something absent-minded about the way she said it. "You looked quite dreadful lying there by the roadside. It was so fortunate we came by just then. Sir Wilfred"—she turned to Ridden and pressed one of his large red paws—"thank you so much for staying to look after him. I really didn't like the idea of poor Billy staying here alone, trying to cope with things by himself. Toby, it's your own fault; I noticed only the other day that your tires were in a dreadful condition. Oh dear, all these dreadful things that keep happening!" She sat down, panting slightly.

Toby said: "Have the police been here?"

"Oh yes," she said impatiently, "they came. It seems that Tomlinson woman gave them some extraordinary message. But thank heaven they have some sense; their work's just work to them—they don't get it all muddled up with melodrama and sensationalism. They talked to Dr. Mason and seemed perfectly satisfied with what he had to tell them."

"He's ready to give a certificate, is he?"

"Of course. Really, when old ladies of ninety-two die suddenly, their doctors are usually ready to give certificates. I'm sorry your accident doesn't seem to have knocked any sense into your head, Toby."

"Quite so, Mrs. Werth. It's given me a headache, that's all."

"It wasn't an accident," Ridden blurted out. "Some bloke had slashed his tires for him."

Mrs. Werth gasped.

Toby said: "Yes, that's what happened. And now I've got a sort of feeling that I'd like to look at the body of Adeline Bievers. Would you mind?"

He stood up before she answered. She stood up too, small, hunched, and taut.

"Certainly I mind," she said. "That poor old woman

dies in her sleep, and you ask me casually if I mind if you look at the body! The callousness of your tone is simply disgusting."

"It's my opinion," said Toby, "that there's someone around here who's much more callous than I am. But I won't labor the point at the moment." He moved to the door.

"No, no," she cried, "I won't have it! It's cruel; it's indecent. And I can't stand much more of this. John, Ugbrook . . . Violence, murder, suspicion . . . Can't you let that poor old thing die her own death in peace?"

"Oh, what the heck does it matter?" asked Lili suddenly. She had not removed her cigarette from her mouth; it wobbled up and down as she spoke. "Let him take a look at her, and much good may it do him."

Mrs. Werth started to say something, but she stopped uncertainly, looking from Toby to Lili.

Toby said: "Thanks, Lili."

She laughed. As Toby went out her laughter increased. As he started for the stairs the sound of it followed him. Loud peals of that false, theatrical laughter followed him up the stairs and into the room where Mrs. Bievers lay dead.

21

CURTAINS WERE DRAWN; windows were closed. The room was musty and ice cold.

The body of the old woman lay on the bed. A sheet covered it. Toby jerked one of the curtains back to let some light into the room, then he crossed to the bed, turned back the sheet, and looked down at the dead face.

Death looked very natural. It looked more natural, almost, than the effort of life had looked on those aged features.

Thoughtfully Toby replaced the sheet, then he moved slowly round the room. He moved without any appearance of purpose, touching nothing, turning frowningly from table to mantelpiece, mantelpiece to cupboard. The room had the characteristic smell of a place that has been lived in by a very old person who scarcely ever goes out of it. Mrs. Bievers' belongings, the carefully hoarded trophies of a cramped but long life, filled all available space. Nothing about them held Toby's attention.

Dissatisfied and uneasy, he turned back to the bed. Then once more he started wandering about. It was about twenty minutes before he went downstairs again.

Voices hushed instantly as he came into the sitting room.

Mrs. Werth raised her black eyes and said challengingly: "Well?"

"I'd like to speak to you alone, if I may," he said.

"There's nothing you can't say to all of us," she answered.

"Indeed there is," he said.

She glanced round, then rose and left the room. She led the way down the murky basement stairs to the kitchen. "Well?" she said again. She dropped into the creaking basket chair as if she were very tired.

"I know you're very angry with me," said Toby. "You think I'm interfering in what isn't my business; you think I'm letting my imagination run away with me and that I'm getting a kick out of it. I'm sorry about all that."

"Leave out the apologies," she said. "What is it you want to say to me?"

"I want to explain a few things," he said, "as a—well, to be blunt, as a sort of warning. You see, for Constance's sake, I shall have to explain them to the police. But I thought I'd tell you about them first so that——"

"One moment," she said. "While you were upstairs did you or did you not find any evidence that there was any foul play connected with the death of Mrs. Bievers?"

"I found none whatever."

"Very well then." She started to rise. "There's nothing else to say, is there?"

"There is. I want to tell you why I still don't believe in the naturalness of her death."

"Oh, Toby," she said fretfully, "you can't mean it seriously. It doesn't make sense. There just couldn't be any reason for harming her. No one could think so."

"Someone thought the fact that I knew what she knew sufficient reason for harming me," said Toby. "My accident wasn't in the least accidental. It happened because my tires had been slashed. And the reason they were slashed was that I thought Mrs. Bievers had been murdered and that I knew why."

"You're imagining things," she said.

He went on: "As I said, I'm telling you this as a kind of warning, so that you can't say I've acted without any consideration for friendship. I know you've told a lie yourself on a rather important matter. Soon the police will know it too. Well, I've no particular wish that they should be able to spring it on you as a surprise."

"Thank you," she said, "but I don't know what you're referring to. I daresay I tell as many lies as most people, but they aren't lies that matter."

"I don't imagine you thought this one mattered," said Toby, "or, if you did—well, it isn't important what you thought about it. The point is, you did tell Cust that

Lili arrived here at six o'clock on Wednesday evening."

"But she did."

"No, Mrs. Werth, she didn't."

The basket chair creaked under her as she stirred slightly. "Be careful, Toby. I think you're insinuating some very unpleasant things."

"Perhaps. But the truth of the matter is that Lili didn't arrive here until after dinner, and you had dinner that night at eight."

"She didn't have dinner here, if that's what you mean. But I never told the inspector that she did. She wouldn't stay, because she said it was unfair to plant herself on me for a meal without any warning. So she went and had something at a Corner House, and then we met later to go to the concert. I've told all that to the police."

"You mean you arranged to meet later and go to that concert before she left here?"

"Yes, of course. I'd bought the tickets a few days before, meaning to take Billy, but Billy was ill in bed, so I had a spare ticket."

"You're quite, quite sure of that story? You really want to stick to it?"

Her face wrinkled into lines of anger. "When the truth serves my purposes I see no reason for departing from it."

"But if you'd already arranged with Lili before dinner to give her your spare ticket," said Toby, "*why did you afterward offer it to old Mrs. Bievers?*"

He could see that she had not been prepared for it.

Whatever attack she had been expecting, it had not been from this direction that she had thought it would come. In the silence that followed his question he saw how surprise stiffened the muscles of her face in a rather grotesque grimace. The next moment she was laughing gently.

"Good heavens, how I've underrated you, Toby! That's really very, very ingenious. Oh, it's really neat; it appeals to me; I like it. I half wish I could throw my hand in and start admitting everything. But you see . . . Oh dear, I don't know quite how to put it, because I don't want to hurt your feelings. You see, Toby, an idea like that . . . well, it's very neat, it's very logical, but it *is* rather superficial, isn't it? It doesn't really take any account of the human factor, does it?"

"The human factor?"

"Yes. I quite understand your reasoning. You believe that if I'd already promised the ticket to Lili I'd never have offered it to Mrs. Bievers, and the fact that I did offer it to Mrs. Bievers——"

"You admit that?"

"Of course I admit it. You believe the fact that I offered the ticket to Mrs. Bievers means that I couldn't already have made any arrangement with Lili—that, in other words, I didn't really see Lili until after dinner, and that, in giving her an alibi for the earlier time when Ugbrook was being killed, I was telling lies. Well, as I said, your idea's neat, it's logical, and yet it's quite false, for the simple reason that it doesn't take into account that it was Mrs. Bievers to whom I offered the ticket.

My dear Toby, I knew she couldn't go to the concert with me. But I also knew it'd give her pleasure if I pretended to persuade her. Why, she never left the house, she scarcely ever left her room, except for very occasional little walks in the square on what she called her good days. It was quite an event when she had dinner downstairs, as she did that evening. But, like lots of old people, she loved to make believe that she was still quite active. Poor, dear old thing. Oh, Toby, you're really too, too stupid!" Mrs. Werth's voice suddenly rang with impatience. "Do you seriously believe I'd have dreamed of taking an old woman of ninety-two to a concert on a freezing-cold winter's night like that? That really would have been murder! All I was doing when I offered her the ticket was pleasing her, playing up to her, flattering her."

In the silence that followed the armchair creaked again as Mrs. Werth settled herself back comfortably.

Toby looked down at the floor. His eyes followed a long crack in the worn linoleum.

Mrs. Werth waited, then said: "Well, Toby?"

He glanced up, then down again. "I don't know. You've certainly made my idea sound pretty silly, and yet I somehow feel inclined to say to you just what you've been saying to me. Too neat, too logical. But I don't know. You've knocked a hole in my argument all right, and yet I've still got a feeling that there's something wrong with that alibi of Lili's."

"Are you developing feminine intuitions, Toby?"

"Perhaps."

"Well, I don't think they'll hurt anybody." She laughed. "My dear Toby, I know you're worried sick about Constance and you're just lashing around wildly, trying to find some way of having her freed. I sympathize—believe me, I do really. I even admire it in a way; loyalty's one of the more impressive virtues. But I can't connive at what you're trying to do to Lili. I know that you've as much prejudice against her as you have in Constance's favor. It's one of Lili's misfortunes that she always affects people violently one way or the other, and you happen to be one of the people who don't respond to her kind of charm. Well, I don't blame you; I know you can't help it. But I do think you oughtn't simply to give in to your prejudice and let it blind your judgment. Because you don't like her it's a little extreme to assume she's a murderess. Incidentally"—there was mockery in the dark eyes—"you're remembering, aren't you, that even if you could prove there was something wrong with Lili's alibi, that's not a proof of her guilt?"

"Oh, I'm remembering that, all right."

She pressed his arm. "That's good. And now why don't you go home, Toby? You're looking very pale still, and that bandage isn't at all pretty. Go home and rest. Shall I call you a taxi? You don't really look in a fit state to be walking about. And try not to worry—I mean about Constance."

For the next few minutes Mrs. Werth went motherly. She patted, soothed him, and gave him advice. All the time there was a look on her face as if she were rather pleased with herself. Toby's face, as he left the house, did not suggest that he was experiencing a similar sensation.

He had not let her call him a taxi, yet he hailed one himself at the corner of the square. Darkness, deepened by the fog, had fallen by the time he reached home. Wearily he dragged himself up the stairs to his flat. The pain of some of his bruises had faded; others ached more acutely than ever. His head was muzzy and burning.

George irritated him by saying that he ought to see a doctor.

"I don't want a doctor, I want a telephone," said Toby. "A telephone and then some peace and quiet. I've got to think, I've got to think."

"But you're lookin' pretty bad," said George.

"I'm feeling pretty bad," said Toby.

"Maybe you ought to be in bed," said George.

"And leave you, in your present obliging state of mind, to get Constance out of prison? Thanks." Toby reached for the telephone and growled into it the number he wanted. When he heard a reply he asked for Inspector Cust.

Cust's voice spoke after a moment: "Well, well, Mr. Dyke, so you've taken to finding murders under gooseberry bushes, have you? That was a nice mare's-nest you sent me after with the old lady. Whatever put it into your head that she might have been murdered?"

"Perhaps it was a mare's-nest and perhaps it wasn't," said Toby. "What I want to talk to you about is Miss Crane. Are you still holding her?"

"We are."

"Are you aware that the key of Ugbrook's house, which you found in her bag, was planted on her by Leora Werth?"

There was a pause. "Are you sure of that?" asked Cust, his voice clipped and official.

"Leora admitted it to me, so no doubt she'll admit it to you if you go the right way about it."

"I see. Thank you. I'll check up on that. And now about the old lady . . . ?"

"I tell you, I don't know where I am about the old lady," said Toby. "When I heard she'd died I suddenly remembered something she'd said which seemed to me to bust Lili Lestarke-Toye's alibi, and I made rather a noise about this idea of mine, as a result of which somebody slashed my tires and I had a nice spill on my way up to London. But now it turns out that there was nothing in my idea—nothing, at any rate, that couldn't very easily be explained away. So why the attempt at pushing me under the daisies? It's a little difficult to follow, isn't it?"

"Umm . . . You say you had this accident *after* you'd spread your ideas about the old lady's death?" said Cust. "Your bright ideas might be easier to understand if they'd followed a knock on the head. Because, believe me, there's nothing in them, Mr. Dyke. Mrs. Bievers died because she'd finished with living—that was the only reason."

"Did you take a look at her?"

"Yes, and I didn't notice anything suspicious."

"Neither did I. Just the same, I wish you'd order a

post-mortem. I still think her death was too much of a coincidence."

He heard the irritated click of Cust's tongue. "Listen, how many people d'you think died during the night all over the country? It's a mighty big coincidence all of those people dying on the same night, don't you think? So perhaps I ought to investigate the connection of every one of those deaths with Ugbrook's murder."

"All right, leave it, but don't leave that business of Leora and the key!"

Toby slammed down the telephone.

He stretched himself out on the couch. When George suggested making him a cup of tea Toby merely closed his eyes and turned his head sideways on the cushions. He was feeling, just then, as if he must have been hurt very badly indeed in the accident, and he even had a moment of panic that he had suffered some serious injury, the results of which were still to appear. After that lassitude settled in and emptiness replaced the crowding problems in his brain. For a little he resisted the lassitude and tried to think, but soon sleep got in the way. He slept heavily for about three hours.

When he awoke the room was in darkness. George had turned out the light and left him. Yet Toby was not alone. Someone was sitting in the chair by the fire. The glow of the gas jets lit up a pair of ankles, the hem of a skirt, and one hand resting on the arm of a chair. As Toby stirred, cursing drowsily at the cramping of his limbs, the woman leaned forward. When the red light of the fire fell on her face he saw that it was Constance.

22

"I'M SORRY," she said, "I didn't mean to wake you."

"I don't know that you did," he said. "When did you get here?"

"Only a little while ago. I came straight here when they let me out. So did an obscure individual in very plain clothes who seems inclined to dog my footsteps. I don't think I'm really what you'd call at liberty."

"You soon will be." Toby sat up. For a moment the shadowy room swam round him. As it settled down again he called out: "George, what about some food?"

George replied from somewhere. Toby reached for the light switch, but he had to close his eyes against the sudden light. He repeated: "You soon will be. But we've got some hard thinking to do. Everyone's telling lies, and we've got to find some way of breaking them down."

"You're looking pretty rotten," she told him.

"I'm all right. You know, Constance, this is a queer business. I've got the whole thing sorted out, and yet I can't see how to prove it."

"Perhaps it'd be best not to worry about it," she said. Her voice was very tired. "Things often straighten out of themselves if you leave them alone."

"Not always. In this case it might be actually dangerous. We're dealing with someone of a certain ruthlessness."

"Well, wait till you've had something to eat, then we'll talk it over."

George appeared with a tray in a few minutes. They ate seated round the fire. Afterward George produced coffee. At that stage Toby started to talk again. Though Constance looked dispirited with fatigue and almost uninterested, she tried to fix her attention on what he had to say. George's plump face was dreamy, much as it generally was when he was listening to the cinema organ.

Toby began: "There'll be some surprises in this for you, Constance; there've been some interesting developments since they shut you up. I don't know quite where to start. I can tell you things in the order I found them out, or I can try to make a coherent story of the things themselves in the order they happened. I think, on the whole, that's what I'll find most useful. It'll show up the gaps."

Constance said: "Yes, well . . . ?"

"It's getting on to three years since Lili first came to Carberry Square," said Toby. "She came with her husband and they stayed for over a month. A little over a year later she returned alone; I believe her story was that Snape had been killed in a train smash. She met John, and in the spring of the following year she married him. There"—he pushed his cup aside—"that sets the stage. The drama really begins with the arrival at Carberry Square of a postcard for Lili. Of course she wasn't living there any more, and the card fell into the hands of Leora Werth, who read it and, though it didn't say very much, spotted something very interesting about it. The handwriting happened to be that of Lili's first husband, Snape."

Constance exclaimed. Toby brought the card out of a pocket and handed it to her.

"You see what it says," he went on. "Snape was telling her to go ahead with her marriage and not be afraid that he'd turn up and give her away, since, as a matter of fact, he was thinking of getting married himself."

"But Leora? You say it was Leora who got the card?"

"Yes, it was Leora. I'm afraid none of us has ever taken nearly enough trouble to understand that odd and rather dangerous young woman. Her mother, with the best intentions in the world, has succeeded in warping her character completely. There's something violently possessive about Mrs. Werth's affections which has made her attempt to keep her children entirely to herself. I think Billy's rather enjoyed it: it's ministered to his egotism and mental indolence; his world's so small that nothing can be nearly as important in it as he is himself. But to Leora her mother's maternal greed has meant tyranny and humiliation. She's come to think of herself as thwarted and oppressed. So it was only natural that when that postcard came the first thing it signified to her was power."

"You mean"—Constance was staring fascinated at the card—"she started to blackmail Lili?"

"No," said Toby, "she didn't. She started to blackmail John."

"John!"

"That's right."

In a sudden convulsion of anger Constance cried: "Oh, if I'd known!"

"You see, that's why John's death precipitated everything else," said Toby. "While John was paying the blackmail Lili was all right. But when John died it was another matter."

"But Ugbrook . . . where does Ugbrook come in? D'you mean that Leora and Ugbrook were working together?"

Toby nodded. "But I wouldn't like to have to explain just what the relationship was between them. I've had Leora's description of it, and I'm inclined to think that as far as she knew she was telling me the truth about it. But I also think that her nature's much too repressed for her to be capable of looking at her own motives honestly. She thinks their friendship was pure and beautiful and that she gave him the card simply so that he could disinterestedly compel John to publish some works of genius. But I think really she was trying to purchase Ugbrook's admiration and indebtedness. He'd once given her a platonic kiss, unfortunately seen by Mrs. Werth, who immediately turned him out of the house, and I think Leora's emotions had got stuck at that point. What Ugbrook himself thought about it all I haven't the faintest idea, and anyway, none of this is very important; the important thing is that the two of them realized that John was sufficiently devoted to Lili to be willing to pay heavy blackmail rather than risk having her arrested for bigamy."

"Did Lili know about it?" asked Constance.

"Oh yes," said Toby, "Lili knew about it. What she didn't know was the plan John had worked out to cope with the danger to her once he was dead—because he was expecting to die."

Constance made a smothered sound. Toby looked at her questioningly, but she said nothing.

He went on: "I think this is what his plan was. He made a new will, totally disinheriting Lili and leaving his property equally divided between you, me, and Mrs. Werth. I suppose you haven't been told that, have you? Did you know that you're legally the owner of a third of John's fortune? That doesn't mean that he didn't want Lili to have the money. All he wanted was that we should hold it in trust for her, and he asked us down on Wednesday evening to explain the whole matter to us; that's to say, he asked you and me—and Ugbrook. He probably felt that Mrs. Werth was a bit too old to be involved in the tougher part of the job. I think he was going to confront Ugbrook with the two of us and tell him we knew the whole story and that we had instructions that if he continued his blackmailing after John's death we were to take the matter to the police. You see, the police try to let the victims of blackmail get off as lightly as they can, and with the husband she'd married bigamously no longer alive, Lili probably wouldn't find herself in any very serious trouble. The reason we had to be in charge of her money was so that we could keep a check on whether or not Ugbrook was still trying to bleed her. John knew Lili by then; he knew she was reckless and dishonest, and he knew that as soon as he was dead she'd marry Ridden. Yes, I'm quite sure he knew that. And that marriage would also have been bigamous, and she'd have been more in Ugbrook's clutches than ever. D'you see? I'm afraid I may not be making it very clear. Our job was to see that she didn't commit any more bigamy or pay any more blackmail. Whatever the details of the scheme were, it's obvious John had decided that Lili was a completely irresponsible member of society and that she needed some trustees."

"But he was trusting us an awful lot, wasn't he?" said Constance.

"What else could he do?" asked Toby. "He had to trust somebody, because he couldn't put his instructions into any sort of legal form; he couldn't even risk putting them on paper. He'd got to fall back on friendship."

The fingers of one of Constance's hands were wrestling with a loose thread on the upholstered arm of her chair.

"But the murder," she said. "What about the murder?"

"Well, on that Wednesday afternoon," said Toby,

"Lili and John had a quarrel, and John rushed out of the house. He was gone some time; he must have walked a lot more than was good for him, and then he actually came home up Hanger Hill. I believe that was the violent exertion that killed him. He must have got home at about a quarter to six, gone up to his room, run a bath, and got undressed—and then died. Died suddenly. Simply fallen down dead. And Lili heard the crash and came up and found him and realized on the spot that here was her chance of getting rid of Ugbrook. She'd only to get him down to Redvers, kill him, and arrange things so that John, who was dead and couldn't suffer for it, should take the blame. Of course she didn't know—she still doesn't know—that Leora was at the back of Ugbrook's blackmailing. She thought that with Ugbrook dead she could safely marry again and become Lady Ridden. She didn't waste much time; a quick thinker, Lili. She went down to the telephone and rang up Ugbrook——"

"No, no, that can't be right," said Constance. "She was at Carberry Square at six. That's one of the things Cust told me."

"It's one of the things that Cust believes," said Toby, "but it isn't true. Unfortunately I haven't yet found the way of proving that it isn't true."

"But how d'you know it isn't?"

"Listen and I'll tell you the rest of the story, then you'll see. She rang up Ugbrook—you can pull my idea to pieces presently—she rang him up and asked him urgently to come down to Redvers *at once*. Probably he'd

been intending to come lateish, like us, but she'd got
to have him arrive before we did. I don't know what
pretext she used; anyway, it worked, and at approximately seven o'clock Ugbrook turned up. In the meantime Lili'd been busy dressing John, dragging him downstairs, and arranging him in the chair at the desk. She'd
also turned on the wireless; I think with the idea that if
any odd noises were heard issuing from the house later,
they'd be taken as part of the program. When Ugbrook
came she let him in. She took him upstairs and he did
a bit of unpacking, smoked a cigarette, then came down.
When he came into the room Lili was waiting for him,
standing behind John. While Ugbrook was still standing
staring she shot at him. As a matter of fact, she shot
twice and missed both times, and that's when the struggle
began. Ugbrook sprang at her and they fought all round
the room——"

"But d'you really think it could have happened like
that?" Constance interrupted. "To make as much havoc
as it did, that struggle must have gone on for some time.
That means two fairly well-matched opponents. I don't
think Ugbrook was a particularly muscular man, but
still he was a man and rather thickset and heavy."

"I've thought about that a good deal," said Toby,
"and I think it could have happened. Lili's tall and well-
made, and her muscles look pretty well developed. If,
as you say, Ugbrook wasn't particularly powerful, I
think she could have held her own against him until she
managed to get hold of the revolver again and put the
third bullet into him."

"All right," said Constance, "go on."

"Well, that's almost the end of it," said Toby, "except for the means she used to persuade Mrs. Werth to give her an alibi. She tidied herself up and, leaving the french windows unlatched on purpose so that it'd be easy for us to get in and discover her nicely set stage, she drove off to London. I suppose she got there sometime after eight and telephoned Mrs. Werth to meet her. They went to the concert, hatched up a story together, and were ready to meet all questions on the subject by the time they received the official news of John's death in the morning."

Constance was frowning. "Then did Lili actually tell Mrs. Werth that she'd killed Ugbrook?"

"No, I'm sure she didn't. I think she told her John had killed him and that all she wanted the alibi for was to save herself from seeming implicated in the killing."

"And you believe Mrs. Werth has told the lies Lili wanted simply out of affection and loyalty?"

"That's what I thought at first. After all, Mrs. Werth was devoted to John and hated Ugbrook. But I've been wondering since whether Lili didn't offer her a more concrete inducement. Suppose Lili knew about the change in John's will—knew about it, that's to say, without understanding the reason for it. It's true she seemed surprised and badly shocked by it yesterday, but she may have been acting up. Suppose she'd told Mrs. Werth about it and promised not to make any attempt to get the will upset if Mrs. Werth would back her up. Lili this morning did a very noble scene of renouncing her claim to John's money, and I've kept puzzling over what made her do it. You see, if she knows she can marry Ridden as soon as she likes, she can afford to part with it."

"And it's true Mrs. Werth has had a hard struggle with poverty for a long time," said Constance thoughtfully. "But does she know that Lili's guilty?"

"I don't think she's quite easy in her mind about it. But even if she were sure that Lili had killed Ugbrook, I doubt if she'd give her away. I wasn't sure about giving her away myself if I could see some other way of getting you clear and while it was only Ugbrook she'd killed. I see no very pressing reason for preserving the lives of blackmailers. But I feel rather different since the death of Adeline Bievers."

George suddenly chuckled. "Say, you do hold on tight to an idea once it gets into your head, Tobe!"

Toby tapped his bandages. "These are what's holding this particular idea in place. As soon as I let out that I believed Mrs. Bievers had been murdered and that I knew why, there was an attempt on my life. So I'm still quite sure Mrs. Bievers was murdered, and I'm still sure the reason was that she was able to destroy Lili's alibi. I thought at first that her knowledge simply consisted of the fact that Mrs. Werth had offered her Billy's ticket for the concert at a time when, according to Mrs. Werth's story, the ticket was already promised to Lili. Well, Mrs. Werth produced an explanation to cover the discrepancy: she said she only offered the ticket to Mrs. Bievers to please her, knowing quite well that the old lady couldn't go out. I don't really believe it, but it's plausible, and it's made me think that Mrs. Bievers must have known something more than I thought; she must have been able to do something really destructive to Lili's alibi. Somehow I've got to find out what it was. If, now that Mrs. Bievers is dead, it's impossible to do that, if her knowledge has really and truly died with her, then I've somehow got to make Mrs. Werth break down."

George reached for the coffeepot and poured out a cup for himself. "There's one thing I don't understand," he said.

Constance asked: "What's that, George?"

"Why did the chicken cross the road?"

"What the devil?" said Toby.

"But I mean it," said George glumly, stirring his coffee.

"Just what do you mean?" asked Constance, smiling.

"Look," said George, "this bloke John Toye, he knows he's got a weak heart; he knows it's goin' to be the finish of him if he ain't careful. And so far as we know he ain't got any idea in his head of committin' suicide. And yet this bloke, after partin' company with Ridden, goes and climbs up Hanger Hill. Now why?"

Constance looked at Toby questioningly. He shrugged.

George went on: "So far as I've been able to follow Toby's description of the countryside, it seems to me that by goin' home along the lower road and up the path through the wood he'd have almost cut out havin' to walk uphill, and it wouldn't have taken him any longer."

Toby nodded. "That's true. But I think there's an

easy answer to your question, George. If John had gone home by the lower road he'd have had to walk most of the way with Ridden."

"M'yes . . . maybe," said George. "Maybe you don't always enjoy walkin' with the bloke that's goin' to marry your wife when you die. Maybe you got it, Tobe. Then there's another thing I been wonderin'. When you was in Sir Wilfred's house did you check up on that musical alibi of his? Did you question his servants to make sure he'd been playin' the what's-it movement from that thing by what's-his-name?"

"No," said Toby, "because it wouldn't have meant anything even if they'd corroborated what he said. He's got a gramophone and records of that sonata; he could have set the thing going and left the house."

"You think people listenin' couldn't have told whether it was him playin' or one of them real clever chaps they put on records? I wish you'd gone into that, Tobe. I wish you'd gone into what was happenin' in his house that evenin'. F'rinstance, did he have any company any of the time? I've got a kind of feelin' that might be important."

"All right," said Toby, "I'll look into it. Have you anything else on your mind, George?"

George nodded, sucking his spoon. "Miss Crane, when you went through Ugbrook's pockets and took out everything you thought'd help to identify him did you notice what he'd got in his pockets? Could you tell me roughly?"

"I think I can, roughly. But I may forget things."

"Well, tell me as near as you can," said George.

"He'd a fountain pen, a cigarette case with a sort of lighter attachment, several pencils, some money, a handkerchief, a notebook, and a lot of the odd letters and scraps of paper people collect in pockets."

"I see," said George thoughtfully. "Thanks, Miss Crane."

"Why did you want to know?" asked Toby.

But George was bunching up his plump features in one hand with a gesture that looked rather as if he had copied it from Inspector Cust.

"What I'd still really like to know," he muttered through his fingers, "is what I said. Why did the chicken cross the road?"

"The usual answer to that question," said Constance, "is that it wanted to get to the other side."

"Ah," said George, "that's just it. You put your finger right on it, Miss Crane. That's just what I been wonderin' about."

23

THERE WAS A THAW in the night. Something also thawed in Toby's brain; a problem that had stayed hard and impenetrable in his mind suddenly dissolved into the simplest of answers.

Toby said to the darkness: "God, what a fool!"

This recognition seemed to give him peace. He slept immediately after it.

He woke late, hearing the drip of melting icicles on the guttering outside. He got up, had a bath, shaved, removed the bandage from his head, and inspected the damage under it. A long cut slanted down the side of his forehead, but the matter was not very serious. He dressed and went in to breakfast.

He said to George: "The whole thing's as clear as daylight."

George took a dubious look out of the window. The

daylight was murky with traces of fog, and the sky was leaden.

"It must have been that knock I got on the head yesterday that made me overlook one of the most obvious things in the whole business," said Toby as he sat down at the table. "I don't know why you didn't spot it yourself. You've usually a very sound instinct about these things."

"Maybe I'm gettin' me baser instincts in hand."

Toby grunted and helped himself to bacon and eggs.

George laid aside the newspaper he had been reading. "The paper says the police are expectin' to make an arrest," he said.

"Why shouldn't they be? It's their job to expect it. George, these eggs are quite dried up."

"Maybe if you'd got up sooner they wouldn't've been. What was it you went and overlooked, Tobe?"

"Ugbrook's car," said Toby.

"Oh," said George, "Ugbrook's car. What about Ugbrook's car?"

"It was in his garage, wasn't it, on the morning after the murder? And yet Ugbrook didn't go down to Mallowby by bus. So what happened?"

"Maybe he got a lift down to Mallowby."

"No. What happened was that the murderer brought the car up to London and put it back in Ugbrook's garage. Don't you see how that gives us a fact we can use? We've only got to check up on one thing and we've got everything we need to have her arrested."

"To have who arrested?"

"Lili, of course. Don't you see, she couldn't have driven two cars at the same time, yet the next morning Ugbrook's car was in its garage and Lili had her own car with her at Carberry Square. She and the Werths drove down in it after I telephoned about John's death. Yet if Ugbrook didn't go down to Mallowby by bus, he must have gone down in his own car, and that means Lili must have driven it back to London. And that means that Lili's car must have been in London that day. If we can prove that, I think the case against her is complete, because if she was at Redvers on Wednesday afternoon, had no car in which to get to London, and didn't travel by bus, then, unless she can produce someone who gave her a lift, she must have gone in Ugbrook's car."

"And suppose she did travel by bus?"

"She didn't. It's very nearly a logical impossibility." Toby reached for the butter. "But I agree that we've got to have proof of it. We'll have to find out whether a conductor on any of the evening buses remembers picking her up at the bus stop near the gates of Redvers. We'll also have to find out where she garaged her car in London. Probably she was having something done to it and we'll find it was at whatever garage she generally goes to."

"And suppose it wasn't; suppose it was in the garage at Redvers all the time?"

"It wasn't," said Toby.

With a frown George looked out at the damp street and slimy pavements.

"Tobe, ain't it occurred to you the murderer may have traveled down to Mallowby with Ugbrook, in Ugbrook's car?" he asked.

Toby looked at him sharply. "Meaning you're thinking of one of the Werths? But all three Werths are remarkably puny people; they'd never have got anywhere in a fight with Ugbrook. Besides, what about the telephone call for Ugbrook just after six, the call from Redvers?"

"Mmm," said George, "yes . . . I was forgettin' about the phone call."

"We'll check up on the buses and we'll check up on Lili's London garage," said Toby, "and we'll find we've got everything. Then we'll get hold of Cust and——"

He stopped as the telephone at his elbow suddenly started ringing.

He reached for it.

A flat, fluty voice spoke to him: "Mr. Dyke? This is Lili Lestarke-Toye speaking."

Toby's dark eyebrows shot up. He winked at George and replied carefully: "Good morning, Mrs. Lestarke-Toye."

"Listen," said Lili, "I've got something I want to say to you."

"Go ahead," said Toby.

"I can't say it now." There was a slight breathlessness in the smooth voice. "I want to see you."

"Where and when?"

"As soon as possible, and wherever we won't be disturbed."

He thought for a moment, then he smiled. "Come here if you like."

"Are you alone?"

He hesitated. "Yes."

"You aren't," she said at once; "you've got somebody with you."

"Well, I can send him away."

"Who is it?"

"Just a friend of mine."

"Is it Inspector Cust?"

"No."

"It's Constance, isn't it?"

"No, it isn't," said Toby; "it's just a friend of no importance, who's got nothing to do with this case, and I can send him away."

A short silence followed, then Lili said: "All right, I'll come, but you're not to have anyone there, d'you understand? I want to speak to you quite privately."

"Private it shall be," said Toby.

"I'll come as soon as I can, but I may not be able to get away immediately. I don't want to attract any attention in coming. So you'll wait for me, won't you?"

Toby said: "Yes, Lili, I'll wait for you."

As she rang off he put his telephone slowly down on its stand and let his breath out in a whistle. Then he went on with his breakfast.

After a few mouthfuls he looked up and said: "George, you'll have to check up on the buses and the garage for me."

George shook his head. "I told you, Tobe, I ain't

havin' nothin' to do with this crime. I'm finished with crime."

"Cut it out! You're going to do this for me. If you think you aren't, I'm going to give you a list of every blessed thing I've ever done for you, and then I'm going to turn you out."

"But, Tobe——"

"There's no time for fooling; this is important. Get along to the bus station and find out which men were on the late buses; find out if any of them remembers picking up a tall, auburn-haired young woman of striking beauty at the bus stop that's just beyond the top of Hanger Hill; after that start inquiries about Lili's car. You may have to go down to Mallowby to get a line on where she usually takes it for repairs. Probably Mrs. Tomlinson, the cook, could tell you something about it. At any rate, don't waste time. I want you to get back as soon as you can. Meanwhile I'm going to be occupied with a conversation that I think may turn out rather—exciting. I've no tires to be slashed, but I've a throat to be cut and various other vulnerable features."

Reluctantly George got to his feet. "Okay, Tobe, I'll do it. Yes, I'll do it. But it's the last time I soil me fingers in this sort of muck."

Toby grinned. "We'll deal with the next case when it arises. Now are you sure you've got it straight? Did Lili get onto any bus——"

"—at the bus stop on Hanger Hill, and also——" But suddenly George stopped. There was a change on his moon of a countenance. "Gorlumme," he said, "now I know why the chicken crossed the road!" Before Toby could say anything he had shot through the door, had snatched an overcoat from a peg, and plunged out onto the staircase.

Toby laughed, then got on with his breakfast. When he had finished he cleared the dishes away and wandered round the room, tidying up odd papers and blowing at some cigarette ash that had sprayed over the table. His efforts did not make much difference to the appearance of the room but seemed to satisfy him. Sitting down, he looked at his watch; it was a quarter to twelve. He picked up the morning paper and settled down to read it while he waited.

At a quarter to one he began to get restless. Crossing to the window, he looked down into the street. The pavements were fairly empty. His gaze ran swiftly over the moving figures, then he went back to the fire, picked up the newspaper again, but after a moment he swore at it and threw it aside. Once more he looked at his watch. For the next half-hour or so he alternately prowled about the room, every now and then looking out of the window, and sat by the fire reading. More and more often he looked at his watch. The hands crept on to half-past one, a quarter to two . . .

When his watch said the time was a minute to two o'clock Toby checked it by switching on the wireless. The wireless was in agreement with his watch. He roamed round the room, occasionally muttering to himself and once picking up the telephone and starting to dial Mrs. Werth's number. But when he had dialed MUS he abandoned the idea. After another couple of turns up and down the carpet he went into the kitchen and cut himself some slices of ham and bread and butter. He found some mustard and some tomatoes, went back to the sitting room, and started to eat.

It was twenty minutes to three when at last the bell rang.

With the sound of it Toby's air of nervousness and uncertainty vanished. He thrust his used plate back into the kitchen and in a couple of silent strides crossed to the hall door, turned the latch noiselessly, and jerked the door open.

In the eyes that met his that sudden, soundless yawning of the door produced a gleam of shock. They were very pale eyes under beetling sandy eyebrows.

"Jove, old man, that startled me!" said Sir Wilfred Ridden.

24

TOBY SAID AFTER A MOMENT: "Sorry. Come in, won't you?"

Ridden said: "Thanks. Glad to see you're better." He followed Toby into the sitting room.

They stood looking at each other.

"Fact is," said Ridden, "I've been doing some thinking. Difficult business, thinking about another person's business—if you see what I mean."

"More or less," said Toby.

"Good. I . . . yes . . . well . . ." Ridden looked about him. "I say, have I butted in or anything? I've sort of got the feeling I came at a bad moment."

"I was expecting somebody else," said Toby.

"Oh, I see. Well, I can go away again if you like. Just say the word."

"No, I think you'd better tell me why you came. I'm

beginning to feel it's probable this other person isn't coming."

"Sure? Well, I'm glad, because now that I've made up my mind about this affair I'd sooner get on with it." Ridden sat down, resting a large red hand on each bony knee. "I tell you, I've been thinking so hard all night my brain feels as if I'd put it through a mangle. It's pretty difficult, thinking for somebody else. I mean, thinking about somebody else's happiness and all that. It's a responsibility; it's taking a lot on oneself. But you seemed to me a pretty reasonable sort of bloke on the whole, so I thought I could come along to you and talk the whole thing over and that that wouldn't be the same thing quite as going straight to the police. Sorry if I don't put it very well, but I expect you see what I'm getting at."

"D'you mean you've decided to give me some facts that you've been holding back from the police?" asked Toby.

"Well . . . yes, that's more or less what it comes to."

"Let me warn you," said Toby, "that I don't promise to treat anything you tell me as confidential."

"Well, I suppose I've just got to accept that," said Ridden, "though I did sort of hope you'd agree to take the thing as just between you and me. But I see your point, of course. Naturally you can't commit yourself. Still, I must say I did sort of hope . . ." He massaged his knees with his large, heavy hands, looking up doubtfully at Toby.

Toby had begun to fill a pipe; he looked down at what he was doing, not at Ridden.

Ridden cleared his throat, then started again abruptly: "First of all, I want you to tell me something, Dyke. No objections to that, I suppose? Is there or is there not any possibility that Lili Lestarke-Toye may be thought guilty of the murder?"

"Why d'you ask?"

"Will you answer my question?"

"Yes, I'll answer it," said Toby, "when you've answered mine. You've had several days when you could have asked yours. What's made it come up at this particular moment?"

"It was something she said to me. It was yesterday evening. She said . . . she said you'd made up your mind she'd killed Ugbrook and that you were so set against her that you'd prove it somehow even though she was innocent."

"But she's got an alibi, hasn't she?" said Toby. "An impeccable alibi."

"Yes, I know," said Ridden unhappily. "But the point is——"

"The alibi's false?"

"Look here, Dyke, I answered your question and you haven't answered mine."

Toby stuck the pipe between his teeth. "Here's your answer, then. Yes, certainly there's a possibility that she may be thought guilty of the murder. At the moment, however, it hasn't been proved. Perhaps it never will be proved. But I've an idea that we'll know the truth in a short time now. If you know anything that'll help her, you shouldn't keep it to yourself."

"I was afraid so," muttered Ridden, "I was afraid so. Good God, it shakes your faith in human nature, doesn't it? Suspecting a girl like Lili—good God, just think of it!"

"I felt inclined to say that when they arrested Constance," said Toby. "It all depends on the point of view."

"She's right," said Ridden, giving him a hard stare, "you're dead set against her. You're convinced she did it. You started out on that assumption, and you've only looked for evidence to back it up. Ah well . . ." He gave a wheezy sigh. "I suppose I'll have to go ahead and tell you what I've got in mind. Fortunately it clears her completely. Probably it was darned foolish of us not to let the thing out straight away, but we never really seriously considered her being suspected. The fact is, Dyke, her alibi *was* false; she didn't spend the first half of the evening with Mrs. Werth—she spent it with me."

"And just why," said Toby, "should you expect me to believe you?"

Ridden blinked at him. He looked like a man who, in broad daylight, walks into a lamppost and whose first instinct seems to be to doubt that the lamppost is there.

"But look here, I've just told you——"

Toby said impatiently: "The time's past when a confession like that had such a guilty sound that it was automatically believed. Can you bring forward any evidence to prove what you've just said?"

"Evidence? I haven't been thinking about evidence,"

said Ridden. "I thought if I just told you what really happened that evening, it'd put things straight."

"So it may, if you can prove it. But we've already had from Mrs. Werth one version of what happened. If you don't mind my saying so, Mrs. Lestarke-Toye seems rather good at finding people who are quite ready to vouch for what happened that evening. By the way, does she know you're here?"

"No," said Ridden, "certainly not. I came on my own responsibility."

"All right," said Toby. "Well, tell me the rest of it."

Ridden squeezed out another sigh. "But if you aren't going to believe me, what's the good? However, here it is. You remember I told you about meeting John down at the bottom of the hill at about half-past five, and how we talked, and then how he went home one way and I went home the other? Well, I suppose it was round about quarter to six when I got home, and there was Lili——"

"Where?"

"At home. Sitting there, waiting for me in the library. She was in a bad state—excited, you know, and worked up. She said she'd already been there about half an hour. She'd——"

"Wait a moment," said Toby. "How did she get in?"

"The usual way, of course. Pearson let her in."

"Pearson?"

"My butler."

"Then can't he corroborate your story for you, or is there some hitch about that?"

Ridden gave another impression of a man walking into a lamppost, but this time he looked as if the solidity of the lamppost were something reassuring to encounter in the flux of doubt and uncertainty.

"Jove, yes, I never thought . . ." But then his jaw dropped. "No, it isn't any good. Pearson knows when she came, but he doesn't know anything about when she left."

"Are you certain of that?"

"You see, she left by the door straight on to the terrace."

"Suppose one of your servants had been listening?"

Ridden's head jerked up. "Good God, I—I hope not!"

"Anyway, when did she leave?" asked Toby.

"Look here, Dyke," said Ridden fretfully, "I want to tell this in my own way." He started massaging his knees again. "I told you when I got home I found Lili there, waiting for me. She was all excited because of a quarrel she'd had with John. She said he still loved Miss Crane better than he did her, and a lot of things like that, and that she was going to leave him. I . . . well, I did what I thought was right; I did my best to calm her down and told her to think it over again and all that sort of thing. I really did do the best I could along that line. It was a bit of an effort because, well, she was crying like the devil, and damn it all, I *wanted* her to leave John —if you see what I mean. She started saying it was obvious I didn't love her either, and that was a bit too much to put up with, so . . . Oh hell, what does it matter what we said or did? But anyway, I did succeed in making her agree to go home again and think the thing over quietly. She left at a few minutes past seven."

"And then you settled down to play Brahms. And was that the last you heard of the matter until Dr. Gayson rang you up from Redvers?"

"No, the next thing I heard was when Lili rang me up from a call box somewhere between here and London," said Ridden. "But I hope I've already made one thing clear: Ugbrook was murdered round seven o'clock or a bit after. Well, Lili might have been there; as I said, she left me soon after seven, and it'd only have taken her a few minutes to run across to Redvers. But she couldn't have been on the spot at the time when the telephone call was made that brought Ugbrook down to Mallowby. That call was made at six o'clock, and at six o'clock she was with me."

"I see." Toby took his pipe out of his mouth and stared at it thoughtfully. "And suppose the telephone call and the murder weren't the work of the same person?"

"But, good God——"

"What did she say when she rang you up on her way to London?" asked Toby.

Ridden seemed to need to collect his wits before he answered. When he spoke it was in a tone of indifference, as if he were still thinking of something else. "She told me about the murder," he said. "I mean, she told me how she'd got back to the house and found John sitting dead at the desk, and Ugbrook on the floor, and the revolver and the bullets . . . Oh, she didn't say much.

She was very upset, of course, and all I really gathered was that I was to stay absolutely quiet about her having been at Mallowby during the evening. She told me she was going to get Mrs. Werth to say she'd been with her since six o'clock. I think if I'd understood the situation better I'd have told her it'd be much wiser to stick to the truth, but all that struck me at the time was that it was probably a good idea to hush up any scandal. Naturally at that time Lili thought John had done the murder, and what she wanted was to fix things so that she didn't get involved in it. She got Mrs. Werth to back her up all right, and I got Pearson to swear he wouldn't say anything about Lili having been at my place, and we thought we were going to get by with it, and then——"

"Then what?" asked Toby as Ridden stopped abruptly.

Ridden pounded on his knees. His voice jumped up several notes: "Then you had to come along with your foul suspicions and your damnable prejudices and start working on Mrs. Werth until you've almost got her believing that Lili's a murderess! Yes, that's what you've done. Mrs. Werth's a darned decent little woman, she's as loyal as they're made, and she told me she'd never once admitted to you that you'd shaken her faith in Lili, but all the same you *have* shaken her—you've made her start wondering whether her conscience'll really let her go on backing up Lili's story. Mrs. Werth came to me and asked me what I thought she ought to do. She swore she still believed in Lili, but I could see how uneasy she was; I could see that if the police gave her a real grilling she'd give way and tell the whole thing. Well, that's why I decided it was best for me to tell the truth about the evening. When things have got to this pass a little scandal doesn't matter. I came to you because I thought it'd be easier talking to you than to the police and that you could then explain to them——"

"Ah, that's just it," said Toby, "what *am* I to explain to them? I'm to explain that both Lili and Mrs. Werth have stubbornly lied about Lili's whereabouts that evening; that your butler Pearson can vouch for her having arrived at your house sometime around half-past five, but that he never saw her leave; that you yourself are ready to swear to the fact that she was at Redvers soon after seven. Taken together with some other things I could explain to the police, I should say it was just putting a rope round her neck. It's true that there's still the telephone call to explain, but there never was any proof that that call was made by the murderer. Mind you, I think it's fairly likely that that rope will go round her neck anyhow, but I don't imagine you'll like the feeling of having had a hand in putting it there. So think pretty carefully before you decide just what you want me to explain to the police."

Ridden's face went dusky. "Oh, I'm to think very carefully, am I? I'm just about putting a rope round her neck? All right, if that's the way you look at it, *I'll tell you what to explain to the police*——"

The bell rang.

Both men started, then Ridden, his voice rising, began again: "I say I'll tell you——"

Toby stopped him. "I shouldn't—not just now. I think that's Mrs. Lestarke-Toye just arrived here; I've been expecting her for some time. She rang up and told me she had something to say to me." He crossed to the door. "I'm not sure how pleased she'll be to find you here."

Ridden got to his feet. "Curse you, you ought to have told me you were expecting her." He stood there, gnawing nervously at his lips, while Toby went out of the room.

Toby opened the hall door. Outside stood Mrs. Werth.

"Toby, what's happened to Lili?" she asked fiercely. "Where is she? What have you done with her?"

25

"You'd better come in," said Toby.

She came into the sitting room. She showed no surprise at seeing Ridden. She looked too absorbed in her own anxiety to think of anything else.

She turned on Toby. "Where's Lili?"

"I'm afraid I don't know," he said.

"You do. She was coming to see you, wasn't she? Where is she?"

"If I could produce her out of a top hat I would, but I haven't a top hat," he answered.

Mrs. Werth looked round her. Her gaze looked piercing and yet at the same time vague, as if she were not really seeing what was before her.

"I'm so worried. I can't think what's happened," she said. "I'm so afraid something may have . . . Oh, it may be completely foolish of me, but such terrible things keep happening. She said she'd only be a short time. Toby, are you sure you haven't seen her? Hasn't she been here at all?"

"I'm afraid not, Mrs. Werth. I've been waiting for her. I've waited rather more than three hours."

"Then she did say she was coming here, did she?"

"Oh yes."

Mrs. Werth sank into a chair. "She wouldn't tell me where she was going, but I'd heard her on the telephone. And that worried me—that she wasn't frank with me. Sir Wilfred, haven't you seen her? Don't you know what's happened to her?"

In the hearty voice that some people mistakenly assume when speaking to someone in need of assurance, he replied: "Oh, you know what Lili is, Mrs. Werth. Temperamental and all that. Probably she simply changed her mind about coming here or perhaps she ran into someone she knew or suddenly decided to go down to Redvers."

"I've rung up Redvers several times," said Mrs. Werth. "I can't get an answer of any kind."

"Oh well, I'm sure she's all right." But Ridden's light-colored eyes shifted uneasily. "What d'you think, Dyke?"

Mrs. Werth ran on: "I know I'm giving in to my fears, but how can one help it? I know you're probably right, Sir Wilfred; she just changed her mind. But, Toby, when she was speaking to you on the telephone she did make it sound urgent, didn't she? She did sound as if there was something very important she wanted to discuss with you?"

"Yes," said Toby, "yes, certainly she did." He stroked his long chin thoughtfully. "However, I'm just beginning to wonder if I didn't fall for that urgency a little too easily."

"What d'you mean?" asked Ridden.

"Suppose she didn't really want to come here at all, but only wanted to make sure I shouldn't go out."

Ridden started to say: "Why——" Then his face went dusky again. He lurched forward a step. "You're at it again, trying to make out all sorts of things against her. Why should she want to make sure you wouldn't go out? I suppose you think she's spending the afternoon committing a whole string of murders. Say it! That's what you think, isn't it? Well, let me tell you something—— Here, what are you going to do?" He grabbed at Toby's arm as Toby picked up the telephone.

Toby started to dial. "I'm going to ring up Cust and tell him that Mrs. Lestarke-Toye is missing."

"Oh no, Toby," said Mrs. Werth, "don't do that. Not yet. Surely it isn't necessary to do that yet. Let's think for a little. Let's think what she could be doing."

Toby kept on with his dialing. "There's no point in delay. If something's happened to her, the sooner the police look into it the better for her. And if she's merely skipped out—well, the sooner they look into it perhaps the better for other people."

Ridden wrenched the telephone away from him. "No, you don't!" He slammed the telephone down on its stand. "I know what you think. You think Lili's guilty of two murders and of an attempted murder and that she's out now probably trying to murder someone else. But you're wrong. I know you're wrong, and I can tell you how I know. I was just telling you, when Mrs. Werth came in, what I wanted you to explain to the police. Well, here it is——"

"You can tell them yourself if I can get in touch with Cust," said Toby. "Give me that telephone."

"No, you don't," said Ridden again as Toby reached for the instrument. But his tone had changed. It had gone quiet and even. He made a sudden movement, and Toby saw an automatic in the other man's hand. "No, you don't, Dyke," said Ridden softly. "Leave that alone and listen to me. And you too, Mrs. Werth—you who began to think that this lunatic here might be right and that Lili—my God, Lili!—might be a murderess. Listen to me, both of you."

He took a step backward toward the door, keeping Toby covered.

"I'll tell you how I know Lili didn't kill Ugbrook. It's very simple." He gave a laugh. "Jove, yes, it's simple! You see, I did it myself. There's your answer. Ha, ha . . . I can see it's taken you by surprise. That's what you can explain to the police in a few minutes, Dyke. You can tell them I'm the man they're looking for. And d'you know why I killed Ugbrook? That's a nice simple one too, though you'd never guess it. I killed him because I thought he was John. And all the time John was sitting there in the dark, looking on at what I was doing—only he was dead. I was busy murdering him, and he was dead all the time—there's a joke for you! A damn good joke!"

"I should think the police'll simply split their sides over it," said Toby, and put out his hand to the telephone again.

Mrs. Werth screamed: "Careful, Toby—oh, be careful!"

"Oh yes, I'd be careful if I were you, Dyke," said Ridden. "You can do all the telephoning you like when I've gone. Of course you'll want me to prove my story. But you don't doubt I wanted to murder John, do you? I tell you, I've been madly in love with Lili ever since I've known her. When she came to me that afternoon and told me how John was treating her I went mad with rage; I made up my mind at once I'd kill him. I sent her up to London, then I set my gramophone going, and I went across to Redvers. I got into the sitting room, which was in darkness, and I waited. Then someone came in, a short, broadish man. I saw him against the window, and I fired. I didn't get him the first time, and he sprang at me and we fought all round the room. After that I switched on the light and saw John sitting there dead. There, that's your story for the police. Go on and tell it—go on and tell it just as I've told you, or I'll put one of these bullets through you!"

Toby was smiling. "And what about the telephone call at six o'clock, the call that brought Ugbrook down to Redvers?"

"You said yourself that might have nothing to do

with the murder, didn't you?" said Ridden. "Well, you were right—it hadn't. I don't know who made it and I don't care. It couldn't have been Lili, because at six o'clock she was at my house."

"It's all very interesting. And that's what you really want me to tell the police?" Toby laughed outright.

At the sound Ridden's finger tightened on the trigger, but at that moment a hand came round from behind him, caught his wrist, and twisted it.

Ridden yelped. The pistol fell out of his hand and clattered on the floor. Shouting and writhing, he tried to get away, but the big, bony man seemed oddly helpless in the grip of the small, pink, plump one who had come in noiselessly through the half-open door.

Mrs. Werth screamed.

Toby said: "Thanks, George—though he wouldn't really have done anything. He's not a killer."

Ridden's chest was heaving. "I tell you, it's true, every word I've told you is true!"

"Gorlumme, what a man'll do for a woman," said George pityingly. He sleeked back his yellow hair. "But don't you worry; she's all right—she's hopped it."

All three turned on him.

Toby snarled: "Hopped it?"

" 'Sright," said George. He straightened his tie. "I tipped her off. I reckoned that was the best thing to do for her. When I left here I waited around, and when she turned up I told her how things stood and pointed out she didn't stand a chance of keeping the bigamy under her hat any longer, and that that meant she wouldn't be able to marry Sir Wilfred here, and also that she might land in jail for a few years if she hung around any longer. Furthermore, I said, if she did hang around, jail might be about the best thing that could happen to her, because with her knowing what she did and gettin' to the state of actually thinkin' of comin' and tellin' you about it, I wouldn't care to guarantee her remainin' here below for more than a few hours. Maybe, I said, she wouldn't even get as far as your door alive. So, bein' a sensible young woman when it don't concern matrimony, she did like I said and hopped it."

"What the hell are you talking about?" asked Toby. He looked a little as if he had been winded. "Didn't you do what I told you?"

"What—you mean about the buses? Yes, course I did, Tobe."

"And did you ask what I told you to ask? Did you ask whether Lili got onto any of those buses on Wednesday evening?"

"No—because I didn't want to waste me breath," said George. "I knew she never traveled up on any of those buses. I knew it because I knew she never done the murder. You was always so prejudiced against her, Tobe—I'm sure I don't know why; she was a bit dumb-like, but she wasn't so bad—you was always so prejudiced you was ready to work your poor brain to death tryin' to make out the evidence pointed at her."

"If you didn't ask what I told you to ask, what did you ask at the bus station?" Toby demanded savagely.

"Why, I simply asked for the conductor of the bus

that got to the top of Hanger Hill at five thirty-five, the bus that Mr. Toye went up the hill to meet. Because, you see, that was why he went all the way up that steep hill. It was to meet the bus. We ought to have thought of that straight away. And then I asked the conductor who it was—— *Look out!*"

But the warning came too late. Perhaps it came intentionally too late.

As George cried out, Mrs. Werth, who had pounced on the automatic as it lay on the floor, pressed it wildly to her own forehead and fired.

26

ON A MONDAY EVENING the small restaurant was nearly empty. Toby and Constance sat at a table in a corner. They kept their voices low.

"But I don't understand," said Constance. "How could it have been Mrs. Werth?"

"That's what I couldn't understand myself at first," said Toby.

"She was so small and thin, she couldn't have been the person who fought with Ugbrook," said Constance. "And what about the hot dinner she dished up for old Mrs. Bievers at eight o'clock? Doesn't a dinner have to be cooked? Besides, what was her motive? Surely she didn't kill him simply because she'd once caught him kissing Leora."

Toby shook his head. "Oh no, her motive was a much

more material one. She was simply eliminating competition. But I'll come round to that presently, and to your other questions. George had an answer to all of them. Really the clue to the whole thing was the spill in the fireplace in Ugbrook's room at Redvers. But I think it'll be best if I start at the very beginning with the actions of John himself during the few days before his death. You see, knowing the probability of his death and wanting to safeguard Lili against Ugbrook and her own recklessness, he'd made the new will, leaving his money divided between you, Mrs. Werth, and me. Then he invited the three of us to go down to Redvers so that he could explain to us what he wanted. Yes, it was Mrs. Werth he invited, not Ugbrook. That letter in which he talked of trust and gratitude wasn't written to the man who'd been blackmailing him. Well, Mrs. Werth couldn't go for the night; she'd got Mrs. Bievers to look after. So she rang John up, telling him she'd come down by the bus arriving at the stop near Redvers at five thirty-five, that she'd hear what he so urgently wanted to say to her, but that she'd got to be home again by eight o'clock to give the old lady her meal. That meal——" Toby gave a short laugh. "You know, I've known what that meal consisted of ever since I went to Carberry Square and had a talk with Billy, but it never struck me it had anything to do with the murder. Mrs. Bievers had stewed chicken and jelly that night. Well, the jelly had obviously been made in the morning, and stewed chicken, so George tells me, can be left to cook for several hours; in fact, if it's a sufficiently aged hen, it *has* to be left for several hours. As to vegetables and so on, I saw the remains of the stew myself, and there were plenty of vegetables in it. Mrs. Werth must have put it on the stove round about four o'clock, then gone to King's Cross and caught the bus down to Mallowby."

"But had she planned the murder already?" asked Constance. "Did she cook up that alibi—I beg your pardon, Toby—on purpose?"

"Oh no, the murder was very impromptu indeed," said Toby. "When she planned that meal she was merely thinking out how she could have the longest possible time for her visit. Well, she got down to Mallowby, and John met her at the bus stop. You remember how George kept asking why John, with his weak heart, went up that hill, when going by the lower road would be much less strenuous? The obvious answer seemed to be that he chose the hill to avoid walking back with Ridden. But the truth was that he went up the hill simply because he wanted to get to the bus stop at the top to meet Mrs. Werth."

At that point the waiter interrupted them, putting plates before them.

"To continue," said Toby. "When John climbed the hill he'd already been walking a good deal more than was good for him, and he had to hurry, because his talk with Ridden had made him late. That was the exertion that killed him a few minutes after he got into the house. But he'd already had a talk with Mrs. Werth by then; they'd talked while they were walking up the drive, and John, who was still wrought up by his quarrel with Lili, had poured out all his troubles. Mrs. Werth had just learned about Lili's bigamy; she knew, too, that Lili was likely to repeat herself as soon as John died, also that Ugbrook had got his claws into her and would batten on her second marriage as he had on her first. Mrs. Werth had also heard about the new will, under which she herself stood to inherit a third of John's property. Of course when they'd got to the house they'd found that Lili and all the servants had cleared out and the place was empty. I imagine Mrs. Werth's brain was in a bit of a whirl as she realized what extraordinary possibilities had opened out before her. I expect she wanted a few minutes to think. Probably it was she who bundled John upstairs to have a bath and change, saying that meanwhile she'd make some tea or something like that. And then she heard a thud. When she got upstairs she found that John was dead." Toby paused, crumbling a piece of bread.

Constance had to say: "And then?" before he went on again.

"Well," said Toby, scraping the crumbs together, "I daresay Mrs. Werth was genuinely fond of John. Perhaps his death was a shock. But when it happened she was pretty quick to see what it could mean to her. She knew that John hadn't yet spoken to you or me and that she herself was the only person apart from Ugbrook—because of course she knew nothing of Leora's part in the business—who knew what Lili had done and why John had left his money as he had. She saw then that if she could eliminate Ugbrook she herself would have control of Lili; she saw that she would be able to force her not to make any appeal against John's will, and later, when Lili had married Ridden, she could be bled steadily and ruthlessly. But if there were the two of them at the game—Mrs. Werth and Ugbrook—then it would be difficult not to overdo things, and the worm might turn. A blackmailer has to know where to draw the line. So Mrs. Werth very rapidly decided to remove Ugbrook and establish a monopoly in dangerous knowledge. She went downstairs, rang him up, giving some reason why he must come to Redvers at once, and then she proceeded to set the stage for his murder."

"She made a good many mistakes, didn't she?" said Constance.

"Oh yes, plenty," said Toby. "She left far too many signs that John hadn't died downstairs, and she left out those things which would have made it seem probable that it was he who had had the fight with Ugbrook. For instance, she didn't scrape any skin off his knuckles or bruise him or disarrange his clothes."

"But that fight," said Constance, frowning. "How could a little, sickly person like Mrs. Werth have fought with Ugbrook?"

"There never was any fight," said Toby. "But there had to be the appearance of a fight to supply a good reason for John's heart failure. It was meant to be very obvious that John had had a fight with Ugbrook, had shot him, and then died himself. I ought to have spotted it straight away. I ought to have spotted that the damage in that room was too overwhelming. Of course what really happened was that when Mrs. Werth had dressed John and dragged him downstairs she systematically wrecked the room. She turned the wireless on to hide the noise. And after she'd done that job she got to work upstairs. You see, she wanted to make it look as if Ugbrook, and not she, had been invited. John, knowing that she was not going to be able to spend the night, had told the servants to get only two rooms ready, so Mrs. Werth had to make a third room look as if it had been prepared for a visitor, putting sheets on the bed and so on. And then she added a touch of overelaboration, another of her mistakes. She took the invitation which John had written to her and which she happened to have in her bag, made a spill out of it, burned off the end which showed to whom the letter had been written, and dropped it on the hearth. Then she put the stub of a cigarette on an ash tray. And it never occurred to her that, having done all that, it'd be wise to go through Ugbrook's pockets after she'd killed him, because, you see, a person very seldom bothers to make a paper spill and light it at an electric heater if he's got a cigarette lighter in his pocket."

"So that's what George was thinking about when he asked me what I'd found in Ugbrook's pockets," said Constance.

"Yes, that was it," said Toby.

"And then she just waited for Ugbrook and shot him?"

"Yes, and then took his suitcase upstairs and unpacked

a few things. And then she got into his car and drove back to London, put it into his garage, walked home, and served up dinner for Mrs. Bievers within a few minutes. But Mrs. Werth had an unpleasant shock when she got home. Mrs. Bievers, who usually stuck to her room, had been having one of her good days and had been prowling about the house. She knew perfectly well that Mrs. Werth had been out all the afternoon."

"So you think Mrs. Werth did kill the old woman?"

"There's going to be a post-mortem," said Toby, "and I feel pretty sure they'll find poison, or possibly a blow at the back of her head. You see, Lili's car *was* taken out in the snow that night, and my tires *were* slashed—and they were slashed just after I'd been making a noise about my being sure that Mrs. Bievers had been murdered and that I knew what it was she knew that had made her murder seem necessary. Actually I was wrong; I didn't know. That's to say, all I knew was that Mrs. Werth had offered the old lady Billy's concert ticket, and that Mrs. Werth very easily and plausibly explained away."

"And what about Lili?"

"Lili, after she'd got rid of the servants, went over to see Ridden. She stayed with him until after seven o'clock. He bribed or bullied his servants into promising to say nothing, but Cust told me this afternoon that one of the servants had talked straight away; it was a parlormaid who'd done a nice evening's eavesdropping and was ready to swear that Lili hadn't left Ridden's library until after seven, so she couldn't possibly have made the telephone call. That didn't mean she couldn't have done the murder, but it did mean she'd have had a very short time in which to arrange John's body downstairs. As a matter of fact, Cust was inclined to believe that it was John himself who'd telephoned, in spite of the operator thinking it was probably a woman's voice she heard. Cust was still banking on finding some conclusive proof that you were guilty."

Constance smiled wryly. "What happened when Lili got back to Redvers?"

"She must have got back," said Toby, "only a few minutes after Mrs. Werth had left in Ugbrook's car. She saw the same scene as you did, and she came to the same conclusion: she believed John had shot Ugbrook. But she was more levelheaded than you. She thought of two things: one was that she must try and keep out of the business herself, and to that end she decided to see if Mrs. Werth would give her a false alibi; the other was that she could take Ugbrook's key and search his flat for the postcard from her husband. I think it was Lili who turned out the light in the room, though that may have been another of Mrs. Werth's mistakes. Mrs. Werth, of course, was only too glad to back up the story that Lili had arrived at Carberry Square at six o'clock, because that backed up her own statement that she hadn't been out of the house all the afternoon. I don't think Lili ever suspected Mrs. Werth of the murder until Ridden blurted out about my tires having been slashed; a minute or two after she'd heard that, Lili suddenly started laughing. It was very strange, very unpleasant laughter. I think it must have been soon after that that Lili decided to come and tell me what she knew. You see, Mrs. Werth had already forced her to do a noble scene of renouncing her right to John's money; probably Mrs. Werth had talked soulfully about her conscience and said she didn't feel able to stick to the story of Lili's having arrived at Carberry Square at six unless Lili made it worth her while. So when Lili heard about my tires she put two and two together . . ."

"Talking of Lili's money," said Constance, "what are we going to do about it?"

"I think we'll hear from Lili in time," said Toby. "She'll probably have a new identity, a new, exotic name —Spanish, perhaps, or Russian—a new shade of hair, and only too probably a new husband. Then we can send her her blasted money. I'm more worried over what to do about Leora and Billy. We'll have to keep an eye on them and do something for them. I'm even mildly worried about Ridden. When I saw him last he was having a sort of breakdown. Hearing about Lili's bigamy seems to have shattered his faith in human nature. He was nearly weeping and saying it was all much more terrible than Aunt Selina's swallowing disinfectant."

Constance gave a dry laugh. Leaning her cheek on her hand, she gazed dreamily before her. She looked tired and unhappy, as if the end of the nightmare had merely left her free to face the fact of John's death.

She said: "I owe you a great deal, Toby."

"You owe George a great deal more," he said. "It's George you'd better thank."

She shook her head. "I think that'd be very tactless. George doesn't like getting mixed up in crime. Toby"— she was looking down at her plate—"I don't think I can eat this. In spite of the name it had on the menu, I'm afraid it's just stewed chicken!"

THE CUP AND THE LIP

ELIZABETH FERRARS

There is nothing unusual about stepping out of your own front door to take a walk.

Except, possibly, in the case of the distinguished novelist Dan Braile. After all, he was not only old but very sick. And it was a wet, stormy evening.

The problems began when he didn't come back. Add to that the fact that several of his friends and family wouldn't have been sorry to see him disappear. Then add to that the claims he'd made that someone was trying to poison him . . .

The mystery deepens when Peter Harkness finds that one of Braile's friends has been shot dead. Deepens for all of them, that is, except the murderer himself . . .

'There are few detective story writers as consistently good as Miss Ferrars'

The Sunday Times

HODDER AND STOUGHTON PAPERBACKS

FILE UNDER: DECEASED

SARAH LACEY

It really wasn't Leah Hunter's lucky day.

True, the handsome stranger in her arms was a bit of a Tom Cruise look-alike. But he was also dead.

Leah, a lively twenty-five year old tax inspector, can't resist a challenge. And when she finds that the dead man's tax records are suspect she delves deeper into what begins to look like a murder case; despite warnings, from the dishy detective sergeant, to stop meddling.

Before long it becomes uncomfortably clear that some-one thinks she knows more than she should. And her Yorkshire town begins to seem an extremely dangerous place to live.

'Sarah has found a real winner in Leah Hunter'
Liza Cody

'A sparky debut; if only the Inland Revenue's one-liners were half as amusing!'
The Observer

HODDER AND STOUGHTON PAPERBACKS

A STRANGE DESIRE

KAY MITCHELL

He was dead before he hit the water. Not a bad way to go. Fast and no regrets.

So why won't his widow accept the Coroner's verdict of a simple heart attack? And why is someone using threats to keep her quiet? And why has the dead man's briefcase mysteriously disappeared?

Chief Inspector Morrissey's investigation reveals that Malminster is not as it seems. When the body of a brutally murdered woman is found to be that of a powerful town official's mistress, Morrissey uncovers some shocking truths exposing an underside of unbridled corruption and conspiracy . . .

HODDER AND STOUGHTON PAPERBACKS

CUT TO THE QUICK

KATE ROSS

Julian Kestrel, debonair dandy of Regency London, finds himself invited to be best man at the wedding of a man he hardly knows and is immediately caught up in the crossfire of the bride and groom's warring families.

The situation rapidly deteriorates when Kestrel finds the dead body of a strange woman tucked into his bed; his valet, a former pickpocket, is accused of the murder.

Who is the victim? How is her death connected to the Fontclair family? And how can Kestrel vindicate his valet without involving the Bow Street Runners?

Probing deep beneath the Fontclairs' respectable surface, Julian Kestrel discovers a trail of secrets, crime and forbidden lust and adds his name to the ranks of great sleuths of ages past.

HODDER AND STOUGHTON PAPERBACKS